Praise for *The Lone Ranger and Tonto Fistfight in Heaven*:

"Poetic [and] unremittingly honest . . . *The Lone Ranger and Tonto Fistfight in Heaven* is for the American Indian what Richard Wright's *Native Son* was for the black American in 1940." —*Chicago Tribune*

"*The Lone Ranger and Tonto Fistfight in Heaven* is a many faceted picture, like a mosaic of broken glass. Reading it is like leaning out the side window of a speeding car, watching the world slip in and out of focus faster than you can sort the future from the present from the past. There is something very hopeful in the very fact Alexie is writing, examining what hurts most, and healing ancient wounds." —*The Washington Post*

"Five hundred years is a long time to wait for a book, but that's how long Indians have been anticipating Sherman Alexie's new collection. Again and again, Alexie's prose startles and dazzles with unexpected, impossible-to-anticipate moves. These are cultural love stories, and we laugh on every page with fist tight around our hearts. With this stunning collection, Sherman Alexie has become quite clearly an important new voice in American literature." —*The Boston Globe*

"Forget the usual stereotypes of a downtrodden people going through the slow motions on some Godforsaken land. There is, to be sure, too much booze and too little hope on the reservation in Alexie's work, but also resilient real people—living and loving, and above all, laughing." —*Seattle Post-Intelligencer*

"Extremely fine . . . Alexie writes with simplicity and forthrightness, allowing the power in his stories to creep up slowly on the reader." —*Publishers Weekly*

"Lyrically beautiful and almost always very funny. Irony, grim humor, and forgiveness help characters transcend pain, anger and loss. The ability both to judge and to love gives this book its searing yet affectionate honesty." —*Kirkus Reviews*

"Alexie blends an almost despairing social realism with jolting flashes of visionary fantasy and a quirky sense of gallows humor. In Sherman Alexie's voice we hear the voice of a people asking questions we cannot answer or avoid."   —*The Bloomsbury Review*

"Alexie writes with grit and lyricism that perfectly capture the absurdity of a proud, dignified people living in squalor, struggling to survive in a society they disdain. Highly recommended."   —*Library Journal*

"[An] impressive collection . . . His tales include all the ingredients of contemporary American Indian life: Humor, heartbreak, and humanity."
                                                                —*Willamette Week*

"Spare, disturbing stories . . . with stark, lyric power."
                                        —*The New York Times Book Review*

"A compelling and impressive collection."   —*The Washington Times*

"Stunning and compelling. Alexie is a visionary and by far the best writer I've seen published in recent years."   —*Talk of the Town* (Washington)

THE LONE RANGER

AND TONTO

FISTFIGHT IN HEAVEN

Also by the Author

Fiction:

Ten Little Indians
The Toughest Indian in the World
Indian Killer
Reservation Blues

Screenplays:

The Business of Fancydancing
Smoke Signals

Poetry:

One Stick Song
The Man Who Loves Salmon
The Summer of Black Widows
Water Flowing Home
Seven Mourning Songs for the Cedar
Flute I Have Yet to Learn to Play
First Indian on the Moon
Old Shirts & New Skins
I Would Steal Horses
The Business of Fancydancing

THE LONE RANGER
AND TONTO
FISTFIGHT IN HEAVEN

Sherman Alexie

GROVE PRESS

NEW YORK

Grateful acknowledgment is made to the following journals, where some of these stories originally appeared, in slightly different form: *Hanging Loose*: "Crazy Horse Dreams" and "Family Portrait"; *Blue Mesa Review*: "Imagining the Reservation"; *Lactuca*: "Amusements"; *Esquire*: "This Is What It Means to Say Phoenix, Arizona."

Printed in the United States of America
Published simultaneously in Canada

Library of Congress Cataloging-in-Publication Data

Alexie, Sherman, 1966–
    The Lone Ranger and Tonto fistfight in heaven / Sherman Alexie.
    ISBN 0-8021-4167-6 (pbk.)
    1. Indians of North America—Fiction. I. Title.
PS3551.L35774L66   1993   813'.54–dc20   93-21780

Design by Laura Hough -

Grove Press
an imprint of Grove/Atlantic, Inc.
841 Broadway
New York, NY 10003

05 06 07 08 09   10 9 8 7 6 5 4 3 2

For Bob, Dick, Mark, and Ron

For Adrian, Joy, Leslie, Simon,

and all those Native writers

whose words and music

have made mine possible

CONTENTS

Introduction   xi

Every Little Hurricane   1

A Drug Called Tradition   12

Because My Father Always Said He Was
the Only Indian Who Saw Jimi Hendrix
Play "The Star-Spangled Banner" at Woodstock   24

Crazy Horse Dreams   37

The Only Traffic Signal on the Reservation
Doesn't Flash Red Anymore   43

Amusements   54

This Is What It Means to Say Phoenix, Arizona   59

The Fun House   76

All I Wanted to Do Was Dance   83

The Trial of Thomas Builds-the-Fire   93

Distances   104

Jesus Christ's Half-Brother Is Alive and Well
on the Spokane Indian Reservation   110

A Train Is an Order of Occurrence
Designed to Lead to Some Result   130

A Good Story   139

The First Annual All-Indian
Horseshoe Pitch and Barbecue   145

Imagining the Reservation   149

The Approximate Size of My Favorite Tumor   154

Indian Education   171

The Lone Ranger and Tonto Fistfight in Heaven   181

Family Portrait   191

Somebody Kept Saying Powwow   199

Witnesses, Secret and Not   211

Flight   224

Junior Polatkin's Wild West Show   232

There's a little bit of magic in everything
and then some loss to even things out.
—Lou Reed

I listen to the gunfire we cannot hear, and begin
this journey with the light of knowing
the root of my own furious love.
—Joy Harjo

INTRODUCTION

In February 1992, Hanging Loose Press of Brooklyn, New York, published my first book of poems and stories, *The Business of Fancydancing,* and I figured it would sell two hundred copies, one hundred and twenty-five of them purchased by my mother. After all, it was a first book by a twenty-six-year-old Spokane Reservation Indian boy from eastern Washington. There was a good chance it would only sell twenty-two copies, seventeen of them purchased by my mother, the formalist, who constantly asked me why my poems didn't rhyme.

"It's free verse," I said. "And some of them do rhyme. I've written sonnets, sestinas, and villanelles. I've written in iambic pentameter."

"What's that?"

"It's the *ba-bump, ba-bump* sound of the heartbeat, of the deer running through the green pine forest, of the eagle singing its way through the sky."

"Don't pull that Indian shaman crap on me," my mother said.

So my mother certainly wasn't impressed by my indigenous rhetoric, but she would have been deliriously happy if I'd become a messianic doctor or lawyer (or a doctor or lawyer with only a messiah complex) and saved the tribe. In a capitalistic sense, that's what the tribe needed (and still needs). But I was a former premedicine major who couldn't handle human anatomy, and I knew far too many lawyers, so I chose the third most lucrative pursuit: small-press poetry.

My family was surprised, but they weren't disappointed. Since I was one of the few people from my tribe to ever go to college, I was already a success story. My mother worked a series of low-wage social-work jobs for the tribe, and my father was a randomly employed blue-collar alcoholic. I made more money delivering pizzas than they did while working far more important jobs. I might have been considered a black sheep if I'd come from a more financially successful family, but my literary ambitions made me a white sheep, albeit a lamb who published in tiny poetry magazines like *The Black Bear Review, Giants Play Well in the Drizzle, Impetus,* and *Slipstream*.

Don't get me wrong. I was excited and proud to be a publishing poet (and still have copies of every journal where I've been published), but I also kept my day job as a program information coordinator (secretary) for People to People, a high school international-exchange program in Spokane. I knew that I would eventually return to college (I left three credits shy of my B.A. in American studies), get that degree, and then trudge through graduate school in creative writing. But I was in no hurry to do that. I just wanted to write my poems (and the occasional story) and live as cheaply as possible. I knew how to live in poverty, having grown up on an American third-world reservation, so my urban six-dollars-an-hour job was almost luxurious.

But a *New York Times Book Review* editor named Rich Nicholls changed my life when he noticed *The Business of Fancydancing* lying in an office slush pile. As he later told me, he thought the cover was extraordinarily beautiful—it featured a surreal photograph of a Navajo fancydancer that some readers wrongly assumed was my self-portrait—and that was the primary reason he picked it up and flipped through the pages. He assigned the book, as well as a few others as part of a survey of contemporary Native American literature, to James Kincaid, an English professor at the University of Southern California. My Hanging Loose editors were shocked to hear one of their books was being reviewed, because there are Pulitzer Prize–winning poets whose books don't get covered in the *Times*. And more shocking, my book was part of a front-page review. Yep, right there on the cover of the *Times Book Review* was a photograph of some Indian guy on a motorcycle (I'm terrified of any vehicle with less than four wheels), and inside that review was Mr. Kincaid declaring me "one of the major lyric voices of our time."

I was sitting at my desk at People to People when my Hanging Loose editor, Bob Hershon, faxed me an advance copy of the review. I read it once, ran to the bathroom to throw up, then returned to my desk to read one sentence again and again: "Mr. Alexie's is one of the major lyric voices of our time."

As Keanu Reeves, the Hawaiian balladeer, would say, "Whoa."

I didn't believe I was one of the major lyric voices of our time (though I'm probably in the top 503 by now), but I guessed that review was going to help my career. In fact, that review tossed my ass over the stadium fence directly into the big leagues. After Kincaid's compliments went public, I started receiving phone calls from agents and editors. Many phone calls. Dozens of calls. A Hollywood producer interrogated me.

"Are the film rights available?" he asked.

"Well, yeah," I said. "But you know it's a book of poems?"

"What do you mean, a book of poems?"

"I mean, poems, you know, with skinny lines, stanzas, mostly free verse, but some rhyming stuff, too. My mom thinks they're pretty cool."

"You mean poem poems?"

"Yes."

"Do your poems tell a story?"

"Most of them are narrative."

"That's good, that's good. Could you send me a copy of the book?"

"You haven't read it?"

"No," he said. "But I read the review. The review was great."

Dozens of agents and editors loved the review (though I wonder how many of them had read the book), and they all wanted to know if I wrote fiction.

"Well," I said to them. "It's not just a book of poetry. There are four short stories in there, too. And a lot of prose poems."

"But do you write fiction?"

"I have a manuscript of short stories. There must be thirty or forty stories in it."

"But do you write fiction?"

I didn't realize that "fiction" was a synonym for "Sure, we'll publish your book of obscure short stories as long as we can also publish your slightly less obscure first novel as part of a two-book deal."

I was terrified by all of these big-time agents and editors, and especially of one particular agent, who enjoyed more fame and fortune than any of her clients did.

"Send me the manuscript today," the famous agent ordered.

Bullied, terrified, and naive, I sent her my manuscript of short stories, glacially printed out by a five-hundred-dollar Brother word processor.

"You're not ready," she said after she'd read them. "I'll take you on as a client, but we're going to have to work on these stories for a year or two before I send them out to publishers."

I was shocked. I had been dreaming about immediate fame and fortune.

"But wait," I said. "I thought I was one of the major lyric voices of our time."

"According to the manuscript I've got sitting in front of me, you're not even one of the major lyric voices on my desk."

Ouch. That one really hurt. And this woman wanted to be my agent? Was that how agents were supposed to talk to their clients? And who the hell was I, calling myself one of the major lyric voices of our time? I was wondering if I should get business cards that identified me as such, or perhaps leave it on my answering machine.

Hello, you've reached Sherman Alexie, one of the major lyric voices of our time. Please leave a message if you're not too intimidated and I'll get back to you, with my versatile and mellifluous voice, as soon as possible.

Of course, these days my wife, Diane, only refers to me as "one of the major lyric voices of our time" when I stutter or mispronounce a word or say something so inane and arrogant that it defies logic. A few years ago, as we argued about the potential danger in using a cracked coffeepot, I shouted, "You can't heat cracked glass! It will shatter! I majored in chemistry! I know glass! What do you know about glass?"

Yep, I have just offered you scientific proof of the majorness of my voice.

"But the thing is," I said to the famous agent. "I think my stories are pretty good. And I hate to be repetitive, but they said I'm one of the major lyric voices of our time."

"These stories are not major. But you've got potential. I'm a great editor. If we take it slow, we can make this book the best it can be."

"I don't know," I said. "I was hoping things would go much faster."

"Going fast would be a mistake for you."

"I don't want to go slow. I can't afford to go slow."

"Then we won't be working together. Call me if you change your mind."

She hung up without saying good-bye. I'd always heard of people who hung up without saying good-bye. I'd seen them on television and in movies, but I'd never talked to somebody who hung up without saying good-bye. She remains the only person I know who has ever hung up on me without saying good-bye.

I still owe her a phone call.

I would love to call her up and say, "Well, Miss Fifteen Percent, we published this book at the speed of the light, and it's now in its 1,220,342nd printing, and it was the basis for a really cool movie called *Smoke Signals*. Maybe you've heard of the movie? It was released by Miramax, yes, *Miramax*, that's spelled M-I-R-A-M-A-X, and the movie won the Audience Award and the Filmmakers' Trophy at the Sundance Film Festival in 1998. Yes, that's *Robert Freaking Redford's Sundance Film Festival!* And I've published one million books since that first one, and I've hugged Stephen King and been kissed on the cheek by Ally Sheedy and sat in a big couch in Kareem Abdul-Jabbar's living room while my feet dangled off the floor, so perhaps you were wrong about EVERYTHING! And by the way, what do you know about glass?"

As they say, revenge is a dish best served with the introduction to the tenth-anniversary edition of a book of short stories.

Eventually, despite my narcissism and naïveté, and thanks to the recommendations of friends, I met the agent Nancy Stauffer Cahoon, who, after reading my manuscript, said something beautiful and surprising.

"That story, 'Flight,' the one about the kid and the jet," she said. "That reminds me of James Tate's poem 'The Lost Pilot.'"

"Wow," I said, falling in literary love. "That story was directly influenced by that poem. Nobody has ever noticed that."

"You had me at hello," Renée Zellweger said to Tom Cruise.

"You had me at James Tate," I said to Nancy.

Okay, I didn't really say that to her. But I was impressed that she talked to me first in artistic terms and only later in financial terms. I hired her immediately (or does the agent hire the writer?), worked with her to edit the manuscript, and immediately cut "Flight" and a dozen other stories. As a sentimental gesture, I've added "Flight" and "Junior Polatkin's Wild West Show" to this edition. I think we deleted "Flight" from the original book because it sounds more like children's literature and "Junior

Polatkin's Wild West Show" because it contains themes more adroitly covered in other stories. Read them for yourself and decide whether we should have kept them.

After Nancy and I got the manuscript into shape, we sent it to twelve or fifteen publishers and set up an auction date. I was going to be auctioned as a literate steer! On a Friday in January 1993, six or eight publishers joined the bidding. During the auction, I updated Bob Hershon, my Hanging Loose god, and Diane, my new girlfriend (and now wife). By the end of the day, Morgan Entrekin and Atlantic Monthly Press had won the auction; then published the book in September 1993. During the twenty-seven-city book tour that followed, I worked with and became friends with, and owe many thanks to, Morgan, Judy Hottensen, Miwa Messer, and Eric Price, my original Dream Team at Grove.

Grove won that original auction with an amount of cash that absolutely boggled my mind. My parents hadn't made that much money in the last ten years combined. I ran outside, jumped into a snowbank, and made angels.

I was rich, rich, rich. Okay, to be more accurate, I was middle-class, middle-class, middle-class. But that was a huge leap. I was the first Alexie to ever become middle-class and all because I wrote stories and poems about being a poor Indian growing up in an alcoholic family on an alcoholic reservation.

This book could have easily been titled *The Lone Ranger and Tonto Get Drunk, Fistfight, and Then Fall into Each Other's Arms and Confess Their Undying Platonic Love for Each Other in Heaven Followed by a Long Evening of Hot Dog Regurgitation and Public Urination.*

When the book was first published, I was (and continue to be) vilified in certain circles for my alcohol-soaked stories. Rereading them, I suppose my critics have a point. Everybody in this book is drunk or in love with a drunk. And in writing about drunk Indians, I am dealing with stereotypical material. But I can only respond with the truth. In my family, counting parents, siblings, and dozens of aunts, uncles, and cousins, there are less than a dozen who are currently sober, and only a few who have never drank. When I write about the destructive effects of alcohol on Indians, I am not writing out of a literary stance or a colonized mind's need to reinforce stereotypes. I am writing autobiography.

When this book was first reviewed, people often commented on its autobiographical nature, and that always pissed me off.

"You see the description on the book," I would say. "It says 'Fiction.' That's what this book is."

Of course, I was full of shit. This book is a thinly disguised memoir. I was a child at the crazy New Year's Eve party depicted in "Every Little Hurricane." My mother did punch another woman in the face during that party. My father and cousin did break through the basement door while playing full-contact Nerf basketball and roll down the stairs together. The best truth about that story is that my mother did stop drinking after that horrible night and has remained sober since. The worst truth? My father never did get sober. He was in residential treatment a few times, attended dozens of AA meetings, took Antabuse, made endless promises to his family and himself, but ended up on dialysis machines during his last years and lost a foot to diabetes before he passed away in March 2003. O my drunk and lovely father! He was one of the Indians who tossed his drunken friend onto the roller coaster in "Amusements." How could one Indian have done such a thing to another Indian? I never asked my father why he did it, but I wrote a story about why I thought it happened, and even after my father read the story, I still didn't have the courage to ask him why he did it. How lame is that?

What else is true? My best friend, Steve, and I traveled to Phoenix to pick up his father's ashes just like Victor and Thomas do in "This Is What It Means to Say Phoenix, Arizona," though the fictional father was much more like my father than Steve's. And yes, there was a flexible gymnast on the airplane during the trip who told Steve and me that she was the first alternate on the 1984 Olympic team. Is that woman out there somewhere? Does she remember two Indian guys sitting across from her on a Morris Air flight from Spokane through Salt Lake City to Phoenix?

A terrified mouse did run up my aunt's pant leg, but I wildly exaggerated the aftermath in "The Fun House." My aunt didn't go swimming in the creek, never felt a need to divorce her husband or leave her son, and she was mad at me for suggesting otherwise.

"Junior," she said. "People are going to think that really happened."

"But it did really happen, Auntie. At least the mouse part. It's a true story."

"Yeah, but it's truer when it's in a book."

"Indian Education" is a true (and truer) account of my public school days. I still have nightmares about missing those two free throws to lose that basketball game against Ritzville. Twenty years later, I can tell you that Doug Wellsandt, Ritzville's star, had just fouled out after he intentionally knocked me to the ground to prevent me from hitting an easy layup. While I stood at the line to shoot the free throws with six seconds on the clock, Ritzville had Keith Humphrey, John Powers, Doug Koch, Miles Curtis, and Jeff McBroom on the court while my teammates—Steve LeBret, Shaun Soliday, John Graham, and Brett Springer—were praying for me to win the game. We had come from sixteen points down in the fourth quarter! It would have been a miracle victory! But I missed those fucking free throws, clanging the ball off the rim twice. Until that point, I had been a 90 percent free-throw shooter. After that night, I was a 50 percent loser. I was a victim of a high school basketball form of Post-Traumatic Free-Throw Stress Syndrome. When I see any of my former teammates now, they still tease me about losing that game. A year after those misses, I hit two free throws and two jump shots in the last minute to win a bigger game against Ritzville, but I never dream about that. Hell, my joy in winning is always much smaller than my pain in losing.

I'm a poet who can whine in meter.

And just like the father-son team in "Witnesses, Secret and Not," my father and I once traveled to Spokane because the police wanted to talk to him about a long-missing and presumed dead Indian man. And yes, my father knew who killed and buried that man, as do most of the people on my reservation. The police know, too, but they can't make a case against the killer. I see that man now and again. He's soft-spoken, funny, and always wears slacks and button-down dress shirts. He once ate dinner at my house while I worried what he might do with his knife and fork. But that's a whole different story, isn't it?

So why am I telling you that these stories are true? First of all, they're not really true. They are the vision of one individual looking at the lives of his family and his entire tribe, so these stories are necessarily biased, incomplete, exaggerated, deluded, and often just plain wrong. But in trying to make them true and real, I am writing what might be called reservation realism.

What is the definition of reservation realism? Well, I'll let you read the book and figure that out for yourself.

As for me, in rereading these stories, some of them written when I was only nineteen years old, I feel like I'm listening to a stranger's dreams. The younger version of me is angrier, more im-pulsive, and deathly afraid of physical description. Every dang In-dian in this book is described as being identically dark skinned, with the same long black hair. It's the Stepford Tribe of Indians. There might be five or six pine trees and a couple of rivers and streams, one grizzly bear and a lot of dogs, but that's about all the flora and fauna you're going to get. It's simple stuff but manages to feel more concentrated rather than sparse. It's funny, too. I laughed a few times at the old jokes, new to me after ten years. But mostly it feels sad, often hopeless, and hot with loneliness. I kept trying to figure out the main topic, the big theme, the overarching idea, the epicenter. And it is this: the sons in this book really love and hate their fathers.

EVERY LITTLE
HURRICANE

Although it was winter, the nearest ocean four hundred miles away, and the Tribal Weatherman asleep because of boredom, a hurricane dropped from the sky in 1976 and fell so hard on the Spokane Indian Reservation that it knocked Victor from bed and his latest nightmare.

It was January and Victor was nine years old. He was sleeping in his bedroom in the basement of the HUD house when it happened. His mother and father were upstairs, hosting the largest New Year's Eve party in tribal history, when the winds increased and the first tree fell.

"Goddamn it," one Indian yelled at another as the argument began. "You ain't shit, you fucking apple."

The two Indians raged across the room at each other. One was tall and heavy, the other was short, muscular. High-pressure and low-pressure fronts.

The music was so loud that Victor could barely hear the voices as the two Indians escalated the argument into a fistfight. Soon there were no voices to be heard, only guttural noises that could have been curses or wood breaking. Then the music stopped so suddenly that the silence frightened Victor.

"What the fuck's going on?" Victor's father yelled, his voice coming quickly and with force. It shook the walls of the house.

"Adolph and Arnold are fighting again," Victor's mother said. Adolph and Arnold were her brothers, Victor's uncles. They always fought. Had been fighting since the very beginning.

"Well, tell them to get their goddamn asses out of my house," Victor's father yelled again, his decibel level rising to meet the tension in the house.

"They already left," Victor's mother said. "They're fighting out in the yard."

Victor heard this and ran to his window. He could see his uncles slugging each other with such force that they had to be in love. Strangers would never want to hurt each other that badly. But it was strangely quiet, like Victor was watching a television show with the volume turned all the way down. He could hear the party upstairs move to the windows, step onto the front porch to watch the battle.

During other hurricanes broadcast on the news, Victor

2

had seen crazy people tie themselves to trees on the beach. Those people wanted to feel the force of the hurricane firsthand, wanted it to be like an amusement ride, but the thin ropes were broken and the people were broken. Sometimes the trees themselves were pulled from the ground and both the trees and the people tied to the trees were carried away.

Standing at his window, watching his uncles grow bloody and tired, Victor pulled the strings of his pajama bottoms tighter. He squeezed his hands into fists and pressed his face tightly against the glass.

"They're going to kill each other," somebody yelled from an upstairs window. Nobody disagreed and nobody moved to change the situation. Witnesses. They were all witnesses and nothing more. For hundreds of years, Indians were witnesses to crimes of an epic scale. Victor's uncles were in the midst of a misdemeanor that would remain one even if somebody was to die. One Indian killing another did not create a special kind of storm. This little kind of hurricane was generic. It didn't even deserve a name.

Adolph soon had the best of Arnold, though, and was trying to drown him in the snow. Victor watched as his uncle held his other uncle down, saw the look of hate and love on his uncle's face and the terrified arms of his other uncle flailing uselessly.

Then it was over.

Adolph let Arnold loose, even pulled him to his feet, and they both stood, facing each other. They started to yell again, unintelligible and unintelligent. The volume grew as other voices from the party upstairs were added. Victor could almost smell the sweat and whiskey and blood.

3

Everybody was assessing the damage, considering options. Would the fight continue? Would it decrease in intensity until both uncles sat quietly in opposite corners, exhausted and ashamed? Could the Indian Health Service doctors fix the broken nose and sprained ankles?

But there was other pain. Victor knew that. He stood at his window and touched his own body. His legs and back hurt from a day of sledding, his head was a little sore from where he bumped into a door earlier in the week. One molar ached from cavity; his chest throbbed with absence.

Victor had seen the news footage of cities after hurricanes had passed by. Houses were flattened, their contents thrown in every direction. Memories not destroyed, but forever changed and damaged. Which is worse? Victor wanted to know if memories of his personal hurricanes would be better if he could change them. Or if he just forgot about all of it. Victor had once seen a photograph of a car that a hurricane had picked up and carried for five miles before it fell onto a house. Victor remembered everything exactly that way.

On Christmas Eve when he was five, Victor's father wept because he didn't have any money for gifts. Oh, there was a tree trimmed with ornaments, a few bulbs from the Trading Post, one string of lights, and photographs of the family with holes punched through the top, threaded with dental floss, and hung from tiny branches. But there were no gifts. Not one.

"But we've got each other," Victor's mother said, but she knew it was just dry recitation of the old Christmas movies they watched on television. It wasn't real. Victor watched his father cry huge, gasping tears. Indian tears.

Victor imagined that his father's tears could have frozen solid in the severe reservation winters and shattered when they hit the floor. Sent millions of icy knives through the air, each specific and beautiful. Each dangerous and random.

Victor imagined that he held an empty box beneath his father's eyes and collected the tears, held that box until it was full. Victor would wrap it in Sunday comics and give it to his mother.

Just the week before, Victor had stood in the shadows of his father's doorway and watched as the man opened his wallet and shook his head. Empty. Victor watched his father put the empty wallet back in his pocket for a moment, then pull it out and open it again. Still empty. Victor watched his father repeat this ceremony again and again, as if the repetition itself could guarantee change. But it was always empty.

During all these kinds of tiny storms, Victor's mother would rise with her medicine and magic. She would pull air down from empty cupboards and make fry bread. She would shake thick blankets free from old bandanas. She would comb Victor's braids into dreams.

In those dreams, Victor and his parents would be sitting in Mother's Kitchen restaurant in Spokane, waiting out a storm. Rain and lightning. Unemployment and poverty. Commodity food. Flash floods.

"Soup," Victor's father would always say. "I want a bowl of soup."

Mother's Kitchen was always warm in those dreams.

There was always a good song on the jukebox, a song that Victor didn't really know but he knew it was good. And he knew it was a song from his parents' youth. In those dreams, all was good.

Sometimes, though, the dream became a nightmare and Mother's Kitchen was out of soup, the jukebox only played country music, and the roof leaked. Rain fell like drums into buckets and pots and pans set out to catch whatever they could. In those nightmares, Victor sat in his chair as rain fell, drop by drop, onto his head.

In those nightmares, Victor felt his stomach ache with hunger. In fact, he felt his whole interior sway, nearly buckle, then fall. Gravity. Nothing for dinner except sleep. Gale and unsteady barometer.

In other nightmares, in his everyday reality, Victor watched his father take a drink of vodka on a completely empty stomach. Victor could hear that near-poison fall, then hit, flesh and blood, nerve and vein. Maybe it was like lightning tearing an old tree into halves. Maybe it was like a wall of water, a reservation tsunami, crashing onto a small beach. Maybe it was like Hiroshima or Nagasaki. Maybe it was like all that. Maybe. But after he drank, Victor's father would breathe in deep and close his eyes, stretch, and straighten his neck and back. During those long drinks, Victor's father wasn't shaped like a question mark. He looked more like an exclamation point.

Some people liked the rain. But Victor hated it. Really hated it. The damp. Humidity. Low clouds and lies. Weathermen. When it was raining, Victor would apologize to everyone he talked to.

6

"Sorry about the weather," he would say.

Once, Victor's cousins made him climb a tall tree during a rainstorm. The bark was slick, nearly impossible to hold on to, but Victor kept climbing. The branches kept most of the rain off him, but there were always sudden funnels of water that broke through, startling enough to nearly make Victor lose his grip. Sudden rain like promises, like treaties. But Victor held on.

There was so much that Victor feared, so much his intense imagination created. For years, Victor feared that he was going to drown while it was raining, so that even when he thrashed through the lake and opened his mouth to scream, he would taste even more water falling from the sky. Sometimes he was sure that he would fall from the top of the slide or from a swing and a whirlpool would suddenly appear beneath him and carry him down into the earth, drown him at the core.

And of course, Victor dreamed of whiskey, vodka, tequila, those fluids swallowing him just as easily as he swallowed them. When he was five years old, an old Indian man drowned in a mud puddle at the powwow. Just passed out and fell facedown into the water collected in a tire track. Even at five, Victor understood what that meant, how it defined nearly everything. Fronts. Highs and lows. Thermals and undercurrents. Tragedy.

When the hurricane descended on the reservation in 1976, Victor was there to record it. If the video camera had been available then, Victor might have filmed it, but his memory was much more dependable.

His uncles, Arnold and Adolph, gave up the fight and

7

walked back into the house, into the New Year's Eve party, arms linked, forgiving each other. But the storm that had caused their momentary anger had not died. Instead, it moved from Indian to Indian at the party, giving each a specific, painful memory.

Victor's father remembered the time his own father was spit on as they waited for a bus in Spokane.

Victor's mother remembered how the Indian Health Service doctor sterilized her moments after Victor was born.

Adolph and Arnold were touched by memories of previous battles, storms that continually haunted their lives. When children grow up together in poverty, a bond is formed that is stronger than most anything. It's this same bond that causes so much pain. Adolph and Arnold reminded each other of their childhood, how they hid crackers in their shared bedroom so they would have something to eat.

"Did you hide the crackers?" Adolph asked his brother so many times that he still whispered that question in his sleep.

Other Indians at the party remembered their own pain. This pain grew, expanded. One person lost her temper when she accidentally brushed the skin of another. The forecast was not good. Indians continued to drink, harder and harder, as if anticipating. There's a fifty percent chance of torrential rain, blizzardlike conditions, seismic activity. Then there's a sixty percent chance, then seventy, eighty.

Victor was back in his bed, lying flat and still, watching the ceiling lower with each step above. The ceiling lowered with the weight of each Indian's pain, until it was just inches from Victor's nose. He wanted to scream, wanted to pretend it was just a nightmare or a game invented by his parents to help him sleep.

8

The voices upstairs continued to grow, take shape and fill space until Victor's room, the entire house, was consumed by the party. Until Victor crawled from his bed and went to find his parents.

"Ya-hey, little nephew," Adolph said as Victor stood alone in a corner.

"Hello, Uncle," Victor said and gave Adolph a hug, gagged at his smell. Alcohol and sweat. Cigarettes and failure.

"Where's my dad?" Victor asked.

"Over there," Adolph said and waved his arm in the general direction of the kitchen. The house was not very large, but there were so many people and so much emotion filling the spaces between people that it was like a maze for little Victor. No matter which way he turned, he could not find his father or mother.

"Where are they?" he asked his aunt Nezzy.

"Who?" she asked.

"Mom and Dad," Victor said, and Nezzy pointed toward the bedroom. Victor made his way through the crowd, hated his tears. He didn't hate the fear and pain that caused them. He expected that. What he hated was the way they felt against his cheeks, his chin, his skin as they made their way down his face. Victor cried until he found his parents, alone, passed out on their bed in the back bedroom.

Victor climbed up on the bed and lay down between them. His mother and father breathed deep, nearly choking alcoholic snores. They were sweating although the room was cold, and Victor thought the alcohol seeping through their skin might get him drunk, might help him sleep. He kissed his mother's neck, tasted the salt and whiskey. He kissed his father's forearm, tasted the cheap beer and smoke.

9

Victor closed his eyes tightly. He said his prayers just in case his parents had been wrong about God all those years. He listened for hours to every little hurricane spun from the larger hurricane that battered the reservation.

During that night, his aunt Nezzy broke her arm when an unidentified Indian woman pushed her down the stairs. Eugene Boyd broke a door playing indoor basketball. Lester FallsApart passed out on top of the stove and somebody turned the burners on high. James Many Horses sat in the corner and told so many bad jokes that three or four Indians threw him out the door into the snow.

"How do you get one hundred Indians to yell *Oh, shit?*" James Many Horses asked as he sat in a drift on the front lawn.

"Say *Bingo,*" James Many Horses answered himself when nobody from the party would.

James didn't spend very much time alone in the snow. Soon Seymour and Lester were there, too. Seymour was thrown out because he kept flirting with all the women. Lester was there to cool off his burns. Soon everybody from the party was out on the lawn, dancing in the snow, fucking in the snow, fighting in the snow.

Victor lay between his parents, his alcoholic and dreamless parents, his mother and father. Victor licked his index finger and raised it into the air to test the wind. Velocity. Direction. Sleep approaching. The people outside seemed so far away, so strange and imaginary. There was a downshift of emotion, tension seemed to wane. Victor put one hand on his mother's stomach and placed the other on his father's. There was enough hunger in both, enough movement, enough geography and history, enough of everything to destroy the reservation and leave only random debris and broken furniture.

But it was over. Victor closed his eyes, fell asleep. It was over. The hurricane that fell out of the sky in 1976 left before sunrise, and all the Indians, the eternal survivors, gathered to count their losses.

A DRUG CALLED TRADITION

"**G**oddamn it, Thomas," Junior yelled. "How come your fridge is always fucking empty?"

Thomas walked over to the refrigerator, saw it was empty, and then sat down inside.

"There," Thomas said. "It ain't empty no more."

Everybody in the kitchen laughed their asses off. It was the second-largest party in reservation history and Thomas Builds-the-Fire was the host. He was the host because he was the one buying all the beer. And he was buying all the beer because he had just got a ton of money from Washington Water Power.

And he just got a ton of money from Washington Water Power because they had to pay for the lease to have ten power poles running across some land that Thomas had inherited.

When Indians make lots of money from corporations that way, we can all hear our ancestors laughing in the trees. But we never can tell whether they're laughing at the Indians or the whites. I think they're laughing at pretty much everybody.

"Hey, Victor," Junior said. "I hear you got some magic mushrooms."

"No way," I said. "Just Green Giant mushrooms. I'm making salad later."

But I did have this brand new drug and had planned on inviting Junior along. Maybe a couple Indian princesses, too. But only if they were full-blood. Well, maybe if they were at least half-Spokane.

"Listen," I whispered to Junior to keep it secret. "I've got some good stuff, a new drug, but just enough for me and you and maybe a couple others. Keep it under your warbonnet."

"Cool," Junior said. "I've got my new car outside. Let's go."

We ditched the party, decided to save the new drug for ourselves, and jumped into Junior's Camaro. The engine was completely shot but the exterior was good. You see, the car looked mean. Mostly we just parked it in front of the Trading Post and tried to look like horsepowered warriors. Driving it was a whole other matter, though. It belched and farted its way down the road like an old man. That definitely wasn't cool.

"Where do you want to go?" Junior asked.

"Benjamin Lake," I said, and we took off in a cloud of oil and exhaust. We drove down the road a little toward Benjamin

13

Lake when we saw Thomas Builds-the-Fire standing by the side of the road. Junior stopped the car and I leaned out the window.

"Hey, Thomas," I asked. "Shouldn't you be at your own party?"

"You guys know it ain't my party anyway," Thomas said. "I just paid for it."

We laughed. I looked at Junior and he nodded his head.

"Hey," I said. "Jump in with us. We're going out to Benjamin Lake to do this new drug I got. It'll be very fucking Indian. Spiritual shit, you know?"

Thomas climbed in back and was just about ready to tell another one of his goddamn stories when I stopped him.

"Now, listen," I said. "You can only come with us if you don't tell any of your stories until after you've taken the drug."

Thomas thought that over awhile. He nodded his head in the affirmative and we drove on. He looked so happy to be spending the time with us that I gave him the new drug.

"Eat up, Thomas," I said. "The party's on me now."

Thomas downed it and smiled.

"Tell us what you see, Mr. Builds-the-Fire," Junior said.

Thomas looked around the car. Hell, he looked around our world and then poked his head through some hole in the wall into another world. A better world.

"Victor," Thomas said. "I can see you. God, you're beautiful. You've got braids and you're stealing a horse. Wait, no. It's not a horse. It's a cow."

Junior almost wrecked because he laughed so hard.

"Why the fuck would I be stealing a cow?" I asked.

"I'm just giving you shit," Thomas said. "No, really, you're stealing a horse and you're riding by moonlight. Van

14

Gogh should've painted this one, Victor. Van Gogh should've painted you."

It was a cold, cold night. I had crawled through the brush for hours, moved by inches so the Others would not hear me. I wanted one of their ponies. I needed one of their ponies. I needed to be a hero and earn my name.

I crawl close enough to their camp to hear voices, to hear an old man sucking the last bit of meat off a bone. I can see the pony I want. He is black, twenty hands high. I can feel him shiver because he knows I have come for him in the middle of this cold night.

Crawling more quickly now, I make my way to the corral, right between the legs of a young boy asleep on his feet. He was supposed to keep watch for men like me. I barely touch his bare leg and he swipes at it, thinking it is a mosquito. If I stood and kissed the young boy full on the mouth, he would only think he was dreaming of the girl who smiled at him earlier in the day.

When I finally come close to the beautiful black pony, I stand up straight and touch his nose, his mane.

I have come for you, I tell the horse, and he moves against me, knows it is true. I mount him and ride silently through the camp, right in front of a blind man who smells us pass by and thinks we are just a pleasant memory. When he finds out the next day who we really were, he will remain haunted and crowded the rest of his life.

I am riding that pony across the open plain, in moonlight that makes everything a shadow.

What's your name? I ask the horse, and he rears back on

his hind legs. He pulls air deep into his lungs and rises above the ground.

Flight, he tells me, *my name is Flight.*

"That's what I see," Thomas said. "I see you on that horse."

Junior looked at Thomas in the rearview mirror, looked at me, looked at the road in front of him.

"Victor," Junior said. "Give me some of that stuff."

"But you're driving," I said.

"That'll make it even better," he said, and I had to agree with him.

"Tell us what you see," Thomas said and leaned forward.

"Nothing yet," Junior said.

"Am I still on that horse?" I asked Thomas.

"Oh, yeah."

We came up on the turnoff to Benjamin Lake, and Junior made it into a screaming corner. Just another Indian boy engaged in some rough play.

"Oh, shit," Junior said. "I can see Thomas dancing."

"I don't dance," Thomas said.

"You're dancing and you ain't wearing nothing. You're dancing naked around a fire."

"No, I'm not."

"Shit, you're not. I can see you, you're tall and dark and fucking huge, cousin."

* * *

They're all gone, my tribe is gone. Those blankets they gave us, infected with smallpox, have killed us. I'm the last, the very last, and I'm sick, too. So very sick. Hot. My fever burning so hot.

I have to take off my clothes, feel the cold air, splash the water across my bare skin. And dance. I'll dance a Ghost Dance. I'll bring them back. Can you hear the drums? I can hear them, and it's my grandfather and my grandmother singing. Can you hear them?

I dance one step and my sister rises from the ash. I dance another and a buffalo crashes down from the sky onto a log cabin in Nebraska. With every step, an Indian rises. With every other step, a buffalo falls.

I'm growing, too. My blisters heal, my muscles stretch, expand. My tribe dances behind me. At first they are no bigger than children. Then they begin to grow, larger than me, larger than the trees around us. The buffalo come to join us and their hooves shake the earth, knock all the white people from their beds, send their plates crashing to the floor.

We dance in circles growing larger and larger until we are standing on the shore, watching all the ships returning to Europe. All the white hands are waving good-bye and we continue to dance, dance until the ships fall off the horizon, dance until we are so tall and strong that the sun is nearly jealous. *We dance that way.*

"Junior," I yelled. "Slow down, slow down."

Junior had the car spinning in circles, doing donuts across empty fields, coming too close to fences and lonely trees.

"Thomas," Junior yelled. "You're dancing, dancing hard."

I leaned over and slammed on the brakes. Junior jumped out of the car and ran across the field. I turned the car off and followed him. We'd gotten about a mile down the road toward Benjamin Lake when Thomas came driving by.

"Stop the car," I yelled. and Thomas did just that.

"Where were you going?" I asked him.

"I was chasing you and your horse, cousin."

"Jesus, this shit is powerful," I said and swallowed some. Instantly I saw and heard Junior singing. He stood on a stage in a ribbon shirt and blue jeans. Singing. With a guitar.

Indians make the best cowboys. I can tell you that. I've been singing at the Plantation since I was ten years old and have always drawn big crowds. All the white folks come to hear my songs, my little pieces of Indian wisdom, although they have to sit in the back of the theater because all the Indians get the best tickets for my shows. It's not racism. The Indians just camp out all night to buy tickets. Even the President of the United States, Mr. Edgar Crazy Horse himself, came to hear me once. I played a song I wrote for his great-grandfather, the famous Lakota warrior who helped us win the war against the whites:

> *Crazy Horse, what have you done?*
> *Crazy Horse, what have you done?*
> *It took four hundred years*
> *and four hundred thousand guns*

but the Indians finally won.
Ya-hey, the Indians finally won.

Crazy Horse, are you still singing?
Crazy Horse, are you still singing?
I honor your old songs
and all they keep on bringing
because the Indians keep winning.
Ya-hey, the Indians keep winning.

Believe me, I'm the best guitar player who ever lived. I can make my guitar sound like a drum. More than that, I can make any drum sound like a guitar. I can take a single hair from the braids of an Indian woman and make it sound like a promise come true. *Like a thousand promises come true.*

"Junior," I asked. "Where'd you learn to sing?"

"I don't know how to sing," he said.

We made our way down the road to Benjamin Lake and stood by the water. Thomas sat on the dock with his feet in the water and laughed softly. Junior sat on the hood of his car, and I danced around them both.

After a little bit, I tired out and sat on the hood of the car with Junior. The drug was beginning to wear off. All I could see in my vision of Junior was his guitar. Junior pulled out a can of warm Diet Pepsi and we passed it back and forth and watched Thomas talking to himself.

"He's telling himself stories," Junior said.

"Well," I said. "Ain't nobody else going to listen."

"Why's he like that?" Junior asked. "Why's he always talking about strange shit? Hell, he don't even need drugs."

"Some people say he got dropped on his head when he was little. Some of the old people think he's magic."

"What do you think?"

"I think he got dropped on his head and I think he's magic."

We laughed, and Thomas looked up from the water, from his stories, and smiled at us.

"Hey," he said. "You two want to hear a story?"

Junior and I looked at each other, looked back at Thomas, and decided that it would be all right. Thomas closed his eyes and told his story.

It is now. Three Indian boys are drinking Diet Pepsi and talking out by Benjamin Lake. They are wearing only loincloths and braids. Although it is the twentieth century and planes are passing overhead, the Indian boys have decided to be real Indians tonight.

They all want to have their vision, to receive their true names, their adult names. That is the problem with Indians these days. They have the same names all their lives. Indians wear their names like a pair of bad shoes.

So they decided to build a fire and breathe in that sweet smoke. They have not eaten for days so they know their visions should arrive soon. Maybe they'll see it in the flames or in the wood. Maybe the smoke will talk in Spokane or English. Maybe the cinders and ash will rise up.

The boys sit by the fire and breathe, their visions arrive. They are all carried away to the past, to the moment before any of them took their first drink of alcohol.

The boy Thomas throws the beer he is offered into the garbage. The boy Junior throws his whiskey through a window. The boy Victor spills his vodka down the drain.

Then the boys sing. They sing and dance and drum. They steal horses. I can see them. *They steal horses.*

"You don't really believe that shit?" I asked Thomas.

"Don't need to believe anything. It just is."

Thomas stood up and walked away. He wouldn't even try to tell us any stories again for a few years. We had never been very good to him, even as boys, but he had always been kind to us. When he stopped even looking at me, I was hurt. How do you explain that?

Before he left for good, though, he turned back to Junior and me and yelled at us. I couldn't really understand what he was saying, but Junior swore he told us not to slow dance with our skeletons.

"What the hell does that mean?" I asked.

"I don't know," Junior said.

There are things you should learn. Your past is a skeleton walking one step behind you, and your future is a skeleton walking one step in front of you. Maybe you don't wear a watch, but your skeletons do, and they always know what time it is. Now, these skeletons are made of memories, dreams, and voices.

And they can trap you in the in-between, between touching and becoming. But they're not necessarily evil, unless you let them be.

What you have to do is keep moving, keep walking, in step with your skeletons. They ain't ever going to leave you, so you don't have to worry about that. Your past ain't going to fall behind, and your future won't get too far ahead. Sometimes, though, your skeletons will talk to you, tell you to sit down and take a rest, breathe a little. Maybe they'll make you promises, tell you all the things you want to hear.

Sometimes your skeletons will dress up as beautiful Indian women and ask you to slow dance. Sometimes your skeletons will dress up as your best friend and offer you a drink, one more for the road. Sometimes your skeletons will look exactly like your parents and offer you gifts.

But, no matter what they do, keep walking, keep moving. And don't wear a watch. Hell, Indians never need to wear a watch because your skeletons will always remind you about the time. See, it is always now. That's what Indian time is. The past, the future, all of it is wrapped up in the now. That's how it is. *We are trapped in the now.*

Junior and I sat out by Benjamin Lake until dawn. We heard voices now and again, saw lights in the trees. After I saw my grandmother walking across the water toward me, I threw away the rest of my new drug and hid in the backseat of Junior's car.

Later that day we were parked in front of the Trading Post, gossiping and laughing, talking stories when Big Mom walked up to the car. Big Mom was the spiritual leader of the Spokane Tribe. She had so much good medicine I think she may have been the one who created the earth.

"I know what you saw," Big Mom said.

"We didn't see nothing," I said, but we all knew that I was lying.

Big Mom smiled at me, shook her head a little, and handed me a little drum. It looked like it was about a hundred years old, maybe older. It was so small it could fit in the palm of my hand.

"You keep that," she said. "Just in case."

"Just in case of what?" I asked.

"That's my pager. Just give it a tap and I'll be right over," she said and laughed as she walked away.

Now, I'll tell you that I haven't used the thing. In fact, Big Mom died a couple years back and I'm not sure she'd come even if the thing did work. But I keep it really close to me, like Big Mom said, just in case. I guess you could call it the only religion I have, one drum that can fit in my hand, but I think if I played it a little, it might fill up the whole world.

BECAUSE MY FATHER ALWAYS SAID HE WAS THE ONLY INDIAN WHO SAW JIMI HENDRIX PLAY "THE STAR-SPANGLED BANNER" AT WOODSTOCK

During the sixties, my father was the perfect hippie, since all the hippies were trying to be Indians. Because of that, how could anyone recognize that my father was trying to make a social statement?

But there is evidence, a photograph of my father demonstrating in Spokane, Washington, during the Vietnam war. The photograph made it onto the wire service and was reprinted in newspapers throughout the country. In fact, it was on the cover of *Time.*

In the photograph, my father is dressed in bell-bottoms

and flowered shirt, his hair in braids, with red peace symbols splashed across his face like war paint. In his hands my father holds a rifle above his head, captured in that moment just before he proceeded to beat the shit out of the National Guard private lying prone on the ground. A fellow demonstrator holds a sign that is just barely visible over my father's left shoulder. It read MAKE LOVE NOT WAR.

The photographer won a Pulitzer Prize, and editors across the country had a lot of fun creating captions and headlines. I've read many of them collected in my father's scrapbook, and my favorite was run in the *Seattle Times*. The caption under the photograph read DEMONSTRATOR GOES TO WAR FOR PEACE. The editors capitalized on my father's Native American identity with other headlines like ONE WARRIOR AGAINST WAR and PEACEFUL GATHERING TURNS INTO NATIVE UPRISING.

Anyway, my father was arrested, charged with attempted murder, which was reduced to assault with a deadly weapon. It was a high-profile case so my father was used as an example. Convicted and sentenced quickly, he spent two years in Walla Walla State Penitentiary. Although his prison sentence effectively kept him out of the war, my father went through a different kind of war behind bars.

"There was Indian gangs and white gangs and black gangs and Mexican gangs," he told me once. "And there was somebody new killed every day. We'd hear about somebody getting it in the shower or wherever and the word would go down the line. Just one word. Just the color of his skin. Red, white, black, or brown. Then we'd chalk it up on the mental scoreboard and wait for the next broadcast."

My father made it through all that, never got into any

serious trouble, somehow avoided rape, and got out of prison just in time to hitchhike to Woodstock to watch Jimi Hendrix play "The Star-Spangled Banner."

"After all the shit I'd been through," my father said, "I figured Jimi must have known I was there in the crowd to play something like that. It was exactly how I felt."

Twenty years later, my father played his Jimi Hendrix tape until it wore down. Over and over, the house filled with the rockets' red glare and the bombs bursting in air. He'd sit by the stereo with a cooler of beer beside him and cry, laugh, call me over and hold me tight in his arms, his bad breath and body odor covering me like a blanket.

Jimi Hendrix and my father became drinking buddies. Jimi Hendrix waited for my father to come home after a long night of drinking. Here's how the ceremony worked:

1. I would lie awake all night and listen for the sounds of my father's pickup.
2. When I heard my father's pickup, I would run upstairs and throw Jimi's tape into the stereo.
3. Jimi would bend his guitar into the first note of "The Star-Spangled Banner" just as my father walked inside.
4. My father would weep, attempt to hum along with Jimi, and then pass out with his head on the kitchen table.
5. I would fall asleep under the table with my head near my father's feet.
6. We'd dream together until the sun came up.

The days after, my father would feel so guilty that he would tell me stories as a means of apology.

"I met your mother at a party in Spokane," my father told me once. "We were the only two Indians at the party. Maybe the only two Indians in the whole town. I thought she was so beautiful. I figured she was the kind of woman who could make buffalo walk on up to her and give up their lives. She wouldn't have needed to hunt. Every time we went walking, birds would follow us around. Hell, tumbleweeds would follow us around."

Somehow my father's memories of my mother grew more beautiful as their relationship became more hostile. By the time the divorce was final, my mother was quite possibly the most beautiful woman who ever lived.

"Your father was always half crazy," my mother told me more than once. "And the other half was on medication."

But she loved him, too, with a ferocity that eventually forced her to leave him. They fought each other with the kind of graceful anger that only love can create. Still, their love was passionate, unpredictable, and selfish. My mother and father would get drunk and leave parties abruptly to go home and make love.

"Don't tell your father I told you this," my mother said. "But there must have been a hundred times he passed out on top of me. We'd be right in the middle of it, he'd say *I love you*, his eyes would roll backwards, and then out went his lights. It sounds strange, I know, but those were good times."

I was conceived during one of those drunken nights, half of me formed by my father's whiskey sperm, the other half formed by my mother's vodka egg. I was born a goofy reservation mixed drink, and my father needed me just as much as he needed every other kind of drink.

One night my father and I were driving home in a near-blizzard after a basketball game, listening to the radio. We didn't talk much. One, because my father didn't talk much when he was sober, and two, because Indians don't need to talk to communicate.

"Hello out there, folks, this is Big Bill Baggins, with the late-night classics show on KROC, 97.2 on your FM dial. We have a request from Betty in Tekoa. She wants to hear Jimi Hendrix's version of 'The Star-Spangled Banner' recorded live at Woodstock."

My father smiled, turned the volume up, and we rode down the highway while Jimi led the way like a snowplow. Until that night, I'd always been neutral about Jimi Hendrix. But, in that near-blizzard with my father at the wheel, with the nervous silence caused by the dangerous roads and Jimi's guitar, there seemed to be more to all that music. The reverberation came to mean something, took form and function.

That song made me want to learn to play guitar, not because I wanted to be Jimi Hendrix and not because I thought I'd ever play for anyone. I just wanted to touch the strings, to hold the guitar tight against my body, invent a chord, and come closer to what Jimi knew, to what my father knew.

"You know," I said to my father after the song was over, "my generation of Indian boys ain't ever had no real war to fight. The first Indians had Custer to fight. My great-grandfather had World War I, my grandfather had World War II, you had Vietnam. All I have is video games."

My father laughed for a long time, nearly drove off the road into the snowy fields.

"Shit," he said. "I don't know why you're feeling sorry for yourself because you ain't had to fight a war. You're lucky. Shit, all you had was that damn Desert Storm. Should have called it Dessert Storm because it just made the fat cats get fatter. It was all sugar and whipped cream with a cherry on top. And besides that, you didn't even have to fight it. All you lost during that war was sleep because you stayed up all night watching CNN."

We kept driving through the snow, talked about war and peace.

"That's all there is," my father said. "War and peace with nothing in between. It's always one or the other."

"You sound like a book," I said.

"Yeah, well, that's how it is. Just because it's in a book doesn't make it not true. And besides, why the hell would you want to fight a war for this country? It's been trying to kill Indians since the very beginning. Indians are pretty much born soldiers anyway. Don't need a uniform to prove it."

Those were the kinds of conversations that Jimi Hendrix forced us to have. I guess every song has a special meaning for someone somewhere. Elvis Presley is still showing up in 7-11 stores across the country, even though he's been dead for years, so I figure music just might be the most important thing there is. Music turned my father into a reservation philosopher. Music had powerful medicine.

"I remember the first time your mother and I danced," my father told me once. "We were in this cowboy bar. We were the only real cowboys there despite the fact that we're Indians. We danced to a Hank Williams song. Danced to that real sad one, you know. 'I'm So Lonesome I Could Cry.' Except your mother and I weren't lonesome or crying. We just shuffled along and fell right goddamn down into love."

"Hank Williams and Jimi Hendrix don't have much in common," I said.

"Hell, yes, they do. They knew all about broken hearts," my father said.

"You sound like a bad movie."

"Yeah, well, that's how it is. You kids today don't know shit about romance. Don't know shit about music either. Especially you Indian kids. You all have been spoiled by those drums. Been hearing them beat so long, you think that's all you need. Hell, son, even an Indian needs a piano or guitar or saxophone now and again."

My father played in a band in high school. He was the drummer. I guess he'd burned out on those. Now, he was like the universal defender of the guitar.

"I remember when your father would haul that old guitar out and play me songs," my mother said. "He couldn't play all that well but he tried. You could see him thinking about what chord he was going to play next. His eyes got all squeezed up and his face turned all red. He kind of looked that way when he kissed me, too. But don't tell him I said that."

Some nights I lay awake and listened to my parents' lovemaking. I know white people keep it quiet, pretend they don't ever make love. My white friends tell me they can't even imagine their own parents getting it on. I know exactly what it sounds like when my parents are touching each other. It makes up for knowing exactly what they sound like when they're fighting. Plus and minus. Add and subtract. It comes out just about even.

Some nights I would fall asleep to the sounds of my parents' lovemaking. I would dream Jimi Hendrix. I could see my father standing in the front row in the dark at Woodstock as Jimi Hendrix played "The Star-Spangled Banner." My mother was at home with me, both of us waiting for my father to find his way back home to the reservation. It's amazing to realize I was alive, breathing and wetting my bed, when Jimi was alive and breaking guitars.

I dreamed my father dancing with all these skinny hippie women, smoking a few joints, dropping acid, laughing when the rain fell. And it did rain there. I've seen actual news footage. I've seen the documentaries. It rained. People had to share food. People got sick. People got married. People cried all kinds of tears.

But as much as I dream about it, I don't have any clue about what it meant for my father to be the only Indian who saw Jimi Hendrix play at Woodstock. And maybe he wasn't the only Indian there. Most likely there were hundreds but my father thought he was the only one. He told me that a million times when he was drunk and a couple hundred times when he was sober.

"I was there," he said. "You got to remember this was near the end and there weren't as many people as before. Not nearly as many. But I waited it out. I waited for Jimi."

A few years back, my father packed up the family and the three of us drove to Seattle to visit Jimi Hendrix's grave. We had our photograph taken lying down next to the grave. There isn't a gravestone there. Just one of those flat markers.

Jimi was twenty-eight when he died. That's younger than Jesus Christ when he died. Younger than my father as we stood over the grave.

"Only the good die young," my father said.

"No," my mother said. "Only the crazy people choke to death on their own vomit."

"Why you talking about my hero that way?" my father asked.

"Shit," my mother said. "Old Jesse WildShoe choked to death on his own vomit and he ain't anybody's hero."

I stood back and watched my parents argue. I was used to these battles. When an Indian marriage starts to fall apart, it's even more destructive and painful than usual. A hundred years ago, an Indian marriage was broken easily. The woman or man just packed up all their possessions and left the tipi. There were no arguments, no discussions. Now, Indians fight their way to the end, holding onto the last good thing, because our whole lives have to do with survival.

After a while, after too much fighting and too many angry words had been exchanged, my father went out and bought a motorcycle. A big bike. He left the house often to ride that thing for hours, sometimes for days. He even strapped an old cassette player to the gas tank so he could listen to music. With that bike, he learned something new about running away. He stopped talking as much, stopped drinking as much. He didn't do much of anything except ride that bike and listen to music.

Then one night my father wrecked his bike on Devil's Gap Road and ended up in the hospital for two months. He broke both his legs, cracked his ribs, and punctured a lung. He also lacerated his kidney. The doctors said he could have died easily. In fact, they were surprised he made it through surgery, let alone survived those first few hours when he lay on the road, bleeding. But I wasn't surprised. That's how my father was.

And even though my mother didn't want to be married to him anymore and his wreck didn't change her mind about that, she still came to see him every day. She sang Indian tunes under her breath, in time with the hum of the machines hooked into my father. Although my father could barely move, he tapped his finger in rhythm.

When he had the strength to finally sit up and talk, hold conversations, and tell stories, he called for me.

"Victor," he said. "Stick with four wheels."

After he began to recover, my mother stopped visiting as often. She helped him through the worst, though. When he didn't need her anymore, she went back to the life she had created. She traveled to powwows, started to dance again. She was a champion traditional dancer when she was younger.

"I remember your mother when she was the best traditional dancer in the world," my father said. "Everyone wanted to call her sweetheart. But she only danced for me. That's how it was. She told me that every other step was just for me."

"But that's only half of the dance," I said.

"Yeah," my father said. "She was keeping the rest for herself. Nobody can give everything away. It ain't healthy."

"You know," I said, "sometimes you sound like you ain't even real."

"What's real? I ain't interested in what's real. I'm interested in how things should be."

My father's mind always worked that way. If you don't

33

like the things you remember, then all you have to do is change the memories. Instead of remembering the bad things, remember what happened immediately before. That's what I learned from my father. For me, I remember how good the first drink of that Diet Pepsi tasted instead of how my mouth felt when I swallowed a wasp with the second drink.

Because of all that, my father always remembered the second before my mother left him for good and took me with her. No. I remembered the second before my father left my mother and me. No. My mother remembered the second before my father left her to finish raising me all by herself.

But however memory actually worked, it was my father who climbed on his motorcycle, waved to me as I stood in the window, and rode away. He lived in Seattle, San Francisco, Los Angeles, before he finally ended up in Phoenix. For a while, I got postcards nearly every week. Then it was once a month. Then it was on Christmas and my birthday.

On a reservation, Indian men who abandon their children are treated worse than white fathers who do the same thing. It's because white men have been doing that forever and Indian men have just learned how. That's how assimilation can work.

My mother did her best to explain it all to me, although I understood most of what happened.

"Was it because of Jimi Hendrix?" I asked her.

"Part of it, yeah," she said. "This might be the only marriage broken up by a dead guitar player."

"There's a first time for everything, enit?"

"I guess. Your father just likes being alone more than he likes being with other people. Even me and you."

Sometimes I caught my mother digging through old photo albums or staring at the wall or out the window. She'd get that look on her face that I knew meant she missed my father. Not enough to want him back. She missed him just enough for it to hurt.

On those nights I missed him most I listened to music. Not always Jimi Hendrix. Usually I listened to the blues. Robert Johnson mostly. The first time I heard Robert Johnson sing I knew he understood what it meant to be Indian on the edge of the twenty-first century, even if he was black at the beginning of the twentieth. That must have been how my father felt when he heard Jimi Hendrix. When he stood there in the rain at Woodstock.

Then on the night I missed my father most, when I lay in bed and cried, with that photograph of him beating that National Guard private in my hands, I imagined his motorcycle pulling up outside. I knew I was dreaming it all but I let it be real for a moment.

"Victor," my father yelled. "Let's go for a ride."

"I'll be right down. I need to get my coat on."

I rushed around the house, pulled my shoes and socks on, struggled into my coat, and ran outside to find an empty driveway. It was so quiet, a reservation kind of quiet, where you can hear somebody drinking whiskey on the rocks three miles away. I stood on the porch and waited until my mother came outside.

"Come on back inside," she said. "It's cold."

"No," I said. "I know he's coming back tonight."

My mother didn't say anything. She just wrapped me in

her favorite quilt and went back to sleep. I stood on the porch all night long and imagined I heard motorcycles and guitars, until the sun rose so bright that I knew it was time to go back inside to my mother. She made breakfast for both of us and we ate until we were full.

CRAZY HORSE DREAMS

She tried to stand close to Victor at the fry bread stand, but he moved from open space to open space, between the other Indians eating and drinking, while he hoped the Blackfoot waitress would finally take his order. When he grew tired of the chase, he turned to leave and she was standing there.

"They don't pay you any mind because your hair is too short," she said.

She's too short to be this honest, he thought. Her braids reach down to her waist, but on a tall woman they would be simple, insignificant. She's wearing a fifty-dollar ribbon shirt manufactured by a company in Spokane. He'd read about the Indian grandmother who designs them, each an original, before she sells them for a standard operating fee. He remembered the redheaded bank teller who cashed his check and asked him if he thought her shirt was authentic. Authentic. He stared at this small Indian woman standing in his way and walked past her.

"Hey, One-Braid," she called after him. "Too good for me?"

"No," he said. "Too big."

He walked away, through the sawchips spread over the ground to keep the dust down, down to the stickgame pavilion. He was surprised to see Willie Boyd holding the bones, making gas money for the ride to the next powwow. He dug into his pockets, found a five-dollar bill, and threw it in with Willie. Willie shifted the bones from hand to hand, a Native magician working without mirrors, his hand an inch quicker than the eyes of the old woman sitting on the other side, trying to find the bone with the colored band. The old woman laughed when she guessed wrong, threw a few crumpled bills into the dirt in front of Willie.

"Let it ride all night, Willie," Victor said. "I ain't going nowhere."

It was only the first night of the powwow, everyone had money in their pockets. A five-dollar bill couldn't mean a thing until the end, when the last van heading out of Browning or Poplar had room for only one more. Willie Boyd drove an RV with a television and a refrigerator, with a sunroof that took in all the air. When it mattered, Victor thought, Willie

Boyd would remember that five dollars. Willie Boyd always remembered.

She was standing behind him, again, when he turned to leave.

"You must be a rich man," she said. "Not much of a warrior, though. You keep letting me sneak up on you."

"You don't surprise me," he said. "The Plains Indians had women who rode their horses eighteen hours a day. They could shoot seven arrows consecutively, have them all in the air at the same time. They were the best light cavalry in the history of the world."

"Just my luck," she said. "An educated Indian."

"Yeah," he said. "Reservation University."

They both laughed at the old joke. Every Indian is an alumnus.

"Where you from?" she asked.

"Wellpinit," he said. "I'm a Spokane."

"I should've known. You got those fisherman's hands."

"Ain't no salmon left in our river. Just a school bus and a few hundred basketballs."

"What the hell you talking about?"

"Our basketball team drives into the river and drowns every year," he said. "It's tradition."

She laughed. "You're just a storyteller, ain't you?"

"I'm just telling you things before they happen," he said. "The same things sons and daughters will tell your mothers and fathers."

"Do you ever answer a question straight?"

"Depends on the question," he said.

"Do you want to be my powwow paradise?"

She took him back to her Winnebago. In the dark, on the plastic mattress, she touched his soft belly. His hands moved over her, fancydancers, each going farther away from his body. He was shaking.

"What are you scared of?" she asked.

"Elevators, escalators, revolving doors. Any kind of forced movement."

"You don't have to worry about those kind of things at a powwow."

"That's not true," he said. "We had an Indian conference at the Sheraton Hotel in Spokane last winter. About twenty of us crowded into an elevator to go up to my room and we got stuck between the twelfth and fourteenth floors. Twenty Indians and a little old white elevator man having a heart attack."

"You're lying," she said. "You stole that story."

"What scares you?" he asked. She was quiet. She stared hard at him, trying to find his features among the shadows, formed a picture of him in her mind. But she was wrong. His hair was thinner, more brown than black. His hands were small. Somehow she was still waiting for Crazy Horse.

"I have this dream about playing bingo," she said. "It's a million-dollar blackout and I only need B-6. But the caller announces B-7 and everyone else in the whole damn place is yelling out, *Bingo!*"

"Sounds more like the truth to me," he said as she reached across him and turned on the light.

Victor was surprised. She had grown. She was the most enormous woman he had ever seen. Her hair fell down over her body, an explosion of horses. She was more beautiful than he wanted, more of a child of freeway exits and cable television, a mother to the children who waited outside 7-11 asking him to buy them a case of Coors Light. She sat on the bus traveling uptown to a community college. She sat on the bus traveling toward cities that grew, doubled. There was nothing he could give her father to earn her hand, nothing she would understand, remember.

"What's wrong?" she asked, reaching for the light again, but he stopped her, held her wrist tightly, painfully.

"Why don't you have any scars?" he asked, pulling her face close to his, her braids touching his chest.

"Why do you have so fucking many?" she asked him.

Then she was afraid of the man naked beside her, under her, afraid of that man who was simple in clothes and cowboy boots, a feather in a bottle.

"You're nothing important," he said. "You're just another goddamned Indian like me."

"Wrong," she said, twisting from his grip and sitting up, her arms crossed over her chest. "I'm the best kind of Indian and I'm in bed with my father."

He laughed. She was silent. She thought she could be saved. She thought he could take her hand and owldance her around the circle. She thought she could watch him fancydance, watch his calf muscles grow more and more perfect with each step. She thought he was Crazy Horse.

He got up, pulled on his Levi's, buttoned his red-and-black flannel shirt, the kind some writer called an Indian shirt. He stepped into his cowboy boots, opened the tiny refrigerator, and grabbed a beer.

"You're nothing. You're nothing," he said and left.

Standing in the dark, next to a tipi with blue smoke escaping from the fire inside, he watched the Winnebago. For hours, Victor watched the lights go on and off, on and off. He wished he was Crazy Horse.

THE ONLY TRAFFIC
SIGNAL ON THE
RESERVATION DOESN'T
FLASH RED ANYMORE

"Go ahead," Adrian said. "Pull the trigger."

I held a pistol to my temple. I was sober but wished I was drunk enough to pull the trigger.

"Go for it," Adrian said. "You chickenshit."

While I still held that pistol to my temple, I used my other hand to flip Adrian off. Then I made a fist with my third hand to gather a little bit of courage or stupidity, and wiped sweat from my forehead with my fourth hand.

"Here," Adrian said. "Give me the damn thing."

Adrian took the pistol, put the barrel in his mouth,

smiled around the metal, and pulled the trigger. Then he cussed wildly, laughed, and spit out the BB.

"Are you dead yet?" I asked.

"Nope," he said. "Not yet. Give me another beer."

"Hey, we don't drink no more, remember? How about a Diet Pepsi?"

"That's right, enit? I forgot. Give me a Pepsi."

Adrian and I sat on the porch and watched the reservation. Nothing happened. From our chairs made rockers by unsteady legs, we could see that the only traffic signal on the reservation had stopped working.

"Hey, Victor," Adrian asked. "Now when did that thing quit flashing?"

"Don't know," I said.

It was summer. Hot. But we kept our shirts on to hide our beer bellies and chicken-pox scars. At least, I wanted to hide my beer belly. I was a former basketball star fallen out of shape. It's always kind of sad when that happens. There's nothing more unattractive than a vain man, and that goes double for an Indian man.

"So," Adrian asked. "What you want to do today?"

"Don't know."

We watched a group of Indian boys walk by. I'd like to think there were ten of them. But there were actually only four or five. They were skinny, darkened by sun, their hair long and wild. None of them looked like they had showered for a week.

Their smell made me jealous.

They were off to cause trouble somewhere, I'm sure. Little warriors looking for honor in some twentieth-century vandalism. Throw a few rocks through windows, kick a dog, slash a tire. Run like hell when the tribal cops drove slowly by the scene of the crime.

"Hey," Adrian asked. "Isn't that the Windmaker boy?"

"Yeah," I said and watched Adrian lean forward to study Julius Windmaker, the best basketball player on the reservation, even though he was only fifteen years old.

"He looks good," Adrian said.

"Yeah, he must not be drinking."

"Yet."

"Yeah, yet."

Julius Windmaker was the latest in a long line of reservation basketball heroes, going all the way back to Aristotle Polatkin, who was shooting jumpshots exactly one year before James Naismith supposedly invented basketball.

I'd only seen Julius play a few times, but he had that gift, that grace, those fingers like a goddamn medicine man. One time, when the tribal school traveled to Spokane to play this white high school team, Julius scored sixty-seven points and the Indians won by forty.

"I didn't know they'd be riding horses," I heard the coach of the white team say when I was leaving.

I mean, Julius was an artist, moody. A couple times he walked right off the court during the middle of a game because there wasn't enough competition. That's how he was. Julius could throw a crazy pass, surprise us all, and send it out of bounds. But nobody called it a turnover because we all knew that one of his teammates should've been there to catch the pass. We loved him.

"Hey, Julius," Adrian yelled from the porch. "You ain't shit."

Julius and his friends laughed, flipped us off, and shook their tail feathers a little as they kept walking down the road. They all knew Julius was the best ballplayer on the reservation these days, maybe the best ever, and they knew Adrian was just confirming that fact.

It was easier for Adrian to tease Julius because he never really played basketball. He was more detached about the whole thing. But I used to be quite a ballplayer. Maybe not as good as some, certainly not as good as Julius, but I still felt that ache in my bones, that need to be better than everyone else. It's that need to be the best, that feeling of immortality, that drives a ballplayer. And when it disappears, for whatever reason, that ballplayer is never the same person, on or off the court.

I know when I lost it, that edge. During my senior year in high school we made it to the state finals. I'd been playing like crazy, hitting everything. It was like throwing rocks into the ocean from a little rowboat. I couldn't miss. Then, right before the championship game, we had our pregame meeting in the first-aid room of the college where the tournament was held every year.

It took a while for our coach to show up so we spent the time looking at these first-aid manuals. These books had all kinds of horrible injuries. Hands and feet smashed flat in printing presses, torn apart by lawnmowers, burned and dismembered. Faces that had gone through windshields, dragged over gravel, split open by garden tools. The stuff was disgusting, but we kept looking, flipping through photograph after photograph, trading books, until we all wanted to throw up.

While I looked at those close-ups of death and destruction, I lost it. I think everybody in that room, everybody on the

46

team, lost that feeling of immortality. We went out and lost the championship game by twenty points. I missed every shot I took. I missed everything.

"So," I asked Adrian. "You think Julius will make it all the way?"

"Maybe, maybe."

There's a definite history of reservation heroes who never finish high school, who never finish basketball seasons. Hell, there's been one or two guys who played just a few minutes of one game, just enough to show what they could have been. And there's the famous case of Silas Sirius, who made one move and scored one basket in his entire basketball career. People still talk about it.

"Hey," I asked Adrian. "Remember Silas Sirius?"

"Hell," Adrian said. "Do I remember? I was there when he grabbed that defensive rebound, took a step, and flew the length of the court, did a full spin in midair, and then dunked that fucking ball. And I don't mean it looked like he flew, or it was so beautiful it was almost like he flew. I mean, he flew, period."

I laughed, slapped my legs, and knew that I believed Adrian's story more as it sounded less true.

"Shit," he continued. "And he didn't grow no wings. He just kicked his legs a little. Held that ball like a baby in his hand. And he was smiling. Really. Smiling when he flew. Smiling when he dunked it, smiling when he walked off the court and never came back. Hell, he was still smiling ten years after that."

I laughed some more, quit for a second, then laughed a little longer because it was the right thing to do.

"Yeah," I said. "Silas was a ballplayer."

"Real ballplayer," Adrian agreed.

In the outside world, a person can be a hero one second and a nobody the next. Think about it. Do white people remember the names of those guys who dove into that icy river to rescue passengers from that plane wreck a few years back? Hell, white people don't even remember the names of the dogs who save entire families from burning up in house fires by barking. And, to be honest, I don't remember none of those names either, but a reservation hero is remembered. A reservation hero is a hero forever. In fact, their status grows over the years as the stories are told and retold.

"Yeah," Adrian said. "It's too bad that damn diabetes got him. Silas was always talking about a comeback."

"Too bad, too bad."

We both leaned further back into our chairs. Silence. We watched the grass grow, the rivers flow, the winds blow.

"Damn," Adrian asked. "When did that fucking traffic signal quit working?"

"Don't know."

"Shit, they better fix it. Might cause an accident."

We both looked at each other, looked at the traffic signal, knew that about only one car an hour passed by, and laughed our asses off. Laughed so hard that when we tried to rearrange ourselves, Adrian ended up with my ass and I ended up with his. That looked so funny that we laughed them off again and it took us most of an hour to get them back right again.

Then we heard glass breaking in the distance.

"Sounds like beer bottles," Adrian said.

"Yeah, Coors Light, I think."

"Bottled 1988."

We started to laugh, but a tribal cop drove by and cruised down the road where Julius and his friends had walked earlier.

"Think they'll catch them?" I asked Adrian.

"Always do."

After a few minutes, the tribal cop drove by again, with Julius in the backseat and his friends running behind.

"Hey," Adrian asked. "What did he do?"

"Threw a brick through a BIA pickup's windshield," one of the Indian boys yelled back.

"Told you it sounded like a pickup window," I said.

"Yeah, yeah, a 1982 Chevy."

"With red paint."

"No, blue."

We laughed for just a second. Then Adrian sighed long and deep. He rubbed his head, ran his fingers through his hair, scratched his scalp hard.

"I think Julius is going to go bad," he said.

"No way," I said. "He's just horsing around."

"Maybe, maybe."

It's hard to be optimistic on the reservation. When a glass sits on a table here, people don't wonder if it's half filled or half empty. They just hope it's good beer. Still, Indians have a way of surviving. But it's almost like Indians can easily survive the big stuff. Mass murder, loss of language and land rights. It's the small things that hurt the most. The white waitress who wouldn't take an order, Tonto, the Washington Redskins.

And, just like everybody else, Indians need heroes to help them learn how to survive. But what happens when our heroes don't even know how to pay their bills?

"Shit, Adrian," I said. "He's just a kid."

"Ain't no children on a reservation."

"Yeah, yeah, I've heard that before. Well," I said. "I guess that Julius is pretty good in school, too."

"And?"

"And he wants to maybe go to college."

"Really?"

"Really," I said and laughed. And I laughed because half of me was happy and half of me wasn't sure what else to do.

A year later, Adrian and I sat on the same porch in the same chairs. We'd done things in between, like ate and slept and read the newspaper. It was another hot summer. Then again, summer is supposed to be hot.

"I'm thirsty," Adrian said. "Give me a beer."

"How many times do I have to tell you? We don't drink anymore."

"Shit," Adrian said. "I keep forgetting. Give me a god-damn Pepsi."

"That's a whole case for you today already."

"Yeah, yeah, fuck these substitute addictions."

We sat there for a few minutes, hours, and then Julius Windmaker staggered down the road.

"Oh, look at that," Adrian said. "Not even two in the afternoon and he's drunk as a skunk."

"Don't he have a game tonight?"

"Yeah, he does."

"Well, I hope he sobers up in time."

"Me, too."

I'd only played one game drunk and it was in an all-Indian basketball tournament after I got out of high school. I'd been drinking the night before and woke up feeling kind of sick, so I got drunk again. Then I went out and played a game. I felt disconnected the whole time. Nothing seemed to fit right. Even my shoes, which had fit perfectly before, felt too big for my feet. I couldn't even see the basketball or basket clearly. They were more like ideas. I mean, I knew where they were generally supposed to be, so I guessed at where I should be. Somehow or another, I scored ten points.

"He's been drinking quite a bit, enit?" Adrian asked.

"Yeah, I hear he's even been drinking Sterno."

"Shit, that'll kill his brain quicker than shit."

Adrian and I left the porch that night and went to the tribal school to watch Julius play. He still looked good in his uniform, although he was a little puffy around the edges. But he just wasn't the ballplayer we all remembered or expected. He missed shots, traveled, threw dumb passes that we all knew were dumb passes. By the fourth quarter, Julius sat at the end of the bench, hanging his head, and the crowd filed out, all talking about which of the younger players looked good. We talked about some kid named Lucy in the third grade who already had a nice move or two.

Everybody told their favorite Julius Windmaker stories, too Times like that, on a reservation, a basketball game felt like a funeral and wake all rolled up together.

Back at home, on the porch, Adrian and I sat wrapped in shawls because the evening was kind of cold.

"It's too bad, too bad," I said. "I thought Julius might be the one to make it all the way."

"I told you he wouldn't. I told you so."

"Yeah, yeah. Don't rub it in."

We sat there in silence and remembered all of our heroes, ballplayers from seven generations, all the way back. It hurts to lose any of them because Indians kind of see ballplayers as saviors. I mean, if basketball would have been around, I'm sure Jesus Christ would've been the best point guard in Nazareth. Probably the best player in the entire world. And in the beyond. I just can't explain how much losing Julius Windmaker hurt us all.

"Well," Adrian asked. "What do you want to do tomorrow?"

"Don't know."

"Shit, that damn traffic signal is still broken. Look."

Adrian pointed down the road and he was right. But what's the point of fixing it in a place where the STOP signs are just suggestions?

"What time is it?" Adrian asked.

"I don't know. Ten, I think."

"Let's go somewhere."

"Where?"

"I don't know, Spokane, anywhere. Let's just go."

"Okay," I said, and we both walked inside the house, shut the door, and locked it tight. No. We left it open just a little bit in case some crazy Indian needed a place to sleep. And in the morning we found crazy Julius passed out on the living room carpet.

"Hey, you bum," Adrian yelled. "Get off my floor."

"This is my house, Adrian," I said.

"That's right. I forgot. Hey, you bum, get your ass off Victor's floor."

Julius groaned and farted but he didn't wake up. It really didn't bother Adrian that Julius was on the floor, so he threw an old blanket on top of him. Adrian and I grabbed our morning coffee and went back out to sit on the porch. We had both just about finished our cups when a group of Indian kids walked by, all holding basketballs of various shapes and conditions.

"Hey, look," Adrian said. "Ain't that the Lucy girl?"

I saw that it was, a little brown girl with scarred knees, wearing her daddy's shirt.

"Yeah, that's her," I said.

"I heard she's so good that she plays for the sixth grade boys team."

"Really? She's only in third grade herself, isn't she?"

"Yeah, yeah, she's a little warrior."

Adrian and I watched those Indian children walk down the road, walking toward another basketball game.

"God, I hope she makes it all the way," I said.

"Yeah, yeah," Adrian said, stared into the bottom of his cup, and then threw it across the yard. And we both watched it with all of our eyes, while the sun rose straight up above us and settled down behind the house, watched that cup revolve, revolve, until it came down whole to the ground.

AMUSEMENTS

I lower a frayed rope into the depths and hoist
the same old Indian tears to my eyes. The liquid is pure and
irresistible.
—Adrian C. Louis

After summer heat and too much coat-pocket whiskey, Dirty Joe passed out on the worn grass of the carnival midway and Sadie and I stood over him, looked down at his flat face, a map for all the wars he fought in the Indian bars. Dirty Joe was no warrior in the old sense. He got his name because he cruised the taverns at closing time, drank all the half-empties and never cared who might have left them there.

"What the hell do we do with him?" I asked Sadie.

"Ah, Victor, let's leave the old bastard here," Sadie said,

but we both knew we couldn't leave another Indian passed out in the middle of a white carnival. Then again, we didn't want to carry his temporarily dead body to wherever it was we were headed next.

"We leave him here and he's going to jail for sure," I said.

"Maybe the drunk tank will do him some good," she said, sat down hard on the grass, her hair falling out of the braid. A century ago she might have been beautiful, her face reflected in the river instead of a mirror. But all the years have changed more than the shape of our blood and eyes. We wear fear now like a turquoise choker, like a familiar shawl.

We sat there beside Dirty Joe and watched all the white tourists watch us, laugh, point a finger, their faces twisted with hate and disgust. I was afraid of all of them, wanted to hide behind my Indian teeth, the quick joke.

"Shit," I said. "We should be charging admission for this show."

"Yeah, a quarter a head and we'd be drinking Coors Light for a week."

"For the rest of our lives, enit?"

After a while I started to agree with Sadie about leaving Dirty Joe to the broom and dustpan. I was just about to stand up when I heard a scream behind me, turned quick to find out what the hell was going on, and saw the reason: a miniature roller coaster called the Stallion.

"Sadie," I said. "Let's put him on the roller coaster."

She smiled for the first time in four or five hundred years and got to her feet.

"That's a real shitty thing to do," she said, laughed, grabbed his arms while I got his legs, and we carried him over to the Stallion.

"Hey," I asked the carny. "I'll give you twenty bucks if you let my cousin here ride this thing all day."

The carny looked at me, at Dirty Joe, back at me and smiled.

"He's drunk as a skunk. He might get hurt."

"Shit," I said. "Indians ain't afraid of a little gravity."

"Oh, hell," the carny said. "Why not?"

We loaded Dirty Joe into the last car and checked his pockets for anything potentially lethal. Nothing. Sadie and I stood there and watched Dirty Joe ride a few times around the circle, his head rolling from side to side, back and forth. He looked like an old blanket we gave away.

"Oh, Jesus, Jesus," Sadie screamed, laughed. She leaned on my shoulder and laughed until tears fell. I looked around and saw a crowd had gathered and joined in on the laughter. Twenty or thirty white faces, open mouths grown large and deafening, wide eyes turned toward Sadie and me. They were jury and judge for the twentieth-century fancydance of these court jesters who would pour Thunderbird wine into the Holy Grail.

"Sadie, I think we better get out of here."

"Oh, shit," she said, realizing what we had done. "Let's go."

"Wait, we have to get Dirty Joe."

"We ain't got time," she said and pulled me away from the crowd. We walked fast and did our best to be anything but Indian. Two little redheaded boys ran by, made Indian noises with their mouths, and as I turned to watch them, one pointed his finger at me and shot.

"Bang," he yelled. "You're dead, Indian."

I looked back over to the Stallion, watched Dirty Joe regain consciousness and lift his head and search for something familiar.

"Sadie, he's awake. We got to go get him."

"Go get him yourself," she said and walked away from me. I watched her move against the crowd, the only person not running to see the drunk Indian riding the Stallion. I turned back in time to watch Dirty Joe stumble from the roller coaster and empty his stomach on the platform. The carny yelled something I couldn't hear, pushed Dirty Joe from behind, and sent him tumbling down the stairs face-first into the grass.

The crowd formed a circle around Dirty Joe; some thin man in a big hat counted like Dirty Joe was a fighter on the canvas. Two security guards pushed through the people, using their billy clubs for leverage. One knelt down beside Dirty Joe while the other spoke to the carny. The carny waved his arms wildly, explained his position, and they both turned toward me. The carny pointed, although he didn't have to, and the guard jumped off the platform.

"Okay, chief," he yelled. "Get your ass over here."

I backpedaled, turned and ran, and could hear the guard behind me as I ran down the midway, past a surprised carny into the fun house where I stumbled through a revolving tunnel, jumped a railing, ran through a curtain, and found myself staring at a three-foot-tall reflection.

Crazy mirrors, I thought as the security guard fell from the tunnel, climbed to his feet, and pulled his billy club from his belt.

Crazy mirrors, I thought, the kind that distort your features, make you fatter, thinner, taller, shorter. The kind that make a white man remember he's the master of ceremonies, barking about the Fat Lady, the Dog-Faced Boy, the Indian who offered up another Indian like some treaty.

Crazy mirrors, I thought, the kind that can never change the dark of your eyes and the folding shut of the good part of your past.

THIS IS WHAT IT MEANS
TO SAY PHOENIX,
ARIZONA

J ust after Victor lost his job at the BIA, he also found out that his father had died of a heart attack in Phoenix, Arizona. Victor hadn't seen his father in a few years, only talked to him on the telephone once or twice, but there still was a genetic pain, which was soon to be pain as real and immediate as a broken bone.

Victor didn't have any money. Who does have money on a reservation, except the cigarette and fireworks salespeople? His father had a savings account waiting to be claimed, but Victor needed to find a way to get to Phoenix. Victor's mother was just as poor as he was, and the rest of his family didn't have any use at all for him. So Victor called the Tribal Council.

"Listen," Victor said. "My father just died. I need some money to get to Phoenix to make arrangements."

"Now, Victor," the council said. "You know we're having a difficult time financially."

"But I thought the council had special funds set aside for stuff like this."

"Now, Victor, we do have some money available for the proper return of tribal members' bodies. But I don't think we have enough to bring your father all the way back from Phoenix."

"Well," Victor said. "It ain't going to cost all that much. He had to be cremated. Things were kind of ugly. He died of a heart attack in his trailer and nobody found him for a week. It was really hot, too. You get the picture."

"Now, Victor, we're sorry for your loss and the circumstances. But we can really only afford to give you one hundred dollars."

"That's not even enough for a plane ticket."

"Well, you might consider driving down to Phoenix."

"I don't have a car. Besides, I was going to drive my father's pickup back up here."

"Now, Victor," the council said. "We're sure there is somebody who could drive you to Phoenix. Or is there somebody who could lend you the rest of the money?"

"You know there ain't nobody around with that kind of money."

"Well, we're sorry, Victor, but that's the best we can do."

Victor accepted the Tribal Council's offer. What else could he do? So he signed the proper papers, picked up his check, and walked over to the Trading Post to cash it.

While Victor stood in line, he watched Thomas Builds-the-Fire standing near the magazine rack, talking to himself. Like he always did. Thomas was a storyteller that nobody wanted to listen to. That's like being a dentist in a town where everybody has false teeth.

Victor and Thomas Builds-the-Fire were the same age, had grown up and played in the dirt together. Ever since Victor could remember, it was Thomas who always had something to say.

Once, when they were seven years old, when Victor's father still lived with the family, Thomas closed his eyes and told Victor this story: "Your father's heart is weak. He is afraid of his own family. He is afraid of you. Late at night he sits in the dark. Watches the television until there's nothing but that white noise. Sometimes he feels like he wants to buy a motorcycle and ride away. He wants to run and hide. He doesn't want to be found."

Thomas Builds-the-Fire had known that Victor's father was going to leave, knew it before anyone. Now Victor stood in the Trading Post with a one-hundred-dollar check in his hand, wondering if Thomas knew that Victor's father was dead, if he knew what was going to happen next.

Just then Thomas looked at Victor, smiled, and walked over to him.

"Victor, I'm sorry about your father," Thomas said.

"How did you know about it?" Victor asked.

"I heard it on the wind. I heard it from the birds. I felt it in the sunlight. Also, your mother was just in here crying."

"Oh," Victor said and looked around the Trading Post. All the other Indians stared, surprised that Victor was even talking to Thomas. Nobody talked to Thomas anymore because he told the same damn stories over and over again. Victor was embarrassed, but he thought that Thomas might be able to help him. Victor felt a sudden need for tradition.

"I can lend you the money you need," Thomas said suddenly. "But you have to take me with you."

"I can't take your money," Victor said. "I mean, I haven't hardly talked to you in years. We're not really friends anymore."

"I didn't say we were friends. I said you had to take me with you."

"Let me think about it."

Victor went home with his one hundred dollars and sat at the kitchen table. He held his head in his hands and thought about Thomas Builds-the-Fire, remembered little details, tears and scars, the bicycle they shared for a summer, so many stories.

Thomas Builds-the-Fire sat on the bicycle, waited in Victor's yard. He was ten years old and skinny. His hair was dirty because it was the Fourth of July.

"Victor," Thomas yelled. "Hurry up. We're going to miss the fireworks."

After a few minutes, Victor ran out of his house, jumped the porch railing, and landed gracefully on the sidewalk.

"And the judges award him a 9.95, the highest score of the summer," Thomas said, clapped, laughed.

"That was perfect, cousin," Victor said. "And it's my turn to ride the bike."

Thomas gave up the bike and they headed for the fairgrounds. It was nearly dark and the fireworks were about to start.

"You know," Thomas said. "It's strange how us Indians celebrate the Fourth of July. It ain't like it was *our* independence everybody was fighting for."

"You think about things too much," Victor said. "It's just supposed to be fun. Maybe Junior will be there."

"Which Junior? Everybody on this reservation is named Junior."

And they both laughed.

The fireworks were small, hardly more than a few bottle rockets and a fountain. But it was enough for two Indian boys. Years later, they would need much more.

Afterwards, sitting in the dark, fighting off mosquitoes, Victor turned to Thomas Builds-the-Fire.

"Hey," Victor said. "Tell me a story."

Thomas closed his eyes and told this story: "There were these two Indian boys who wanted to be warriors. But it was too late to be warriors in the old way. All the horses were gone. So the two Indian boys stole a car and drove to the city. They parked the stolen car in front of the police station and then hitchhiked back home to the reservation. When they got back, all their friends cheered and their parents' eyes shone with pride. *You were very brave*, everybody said to the two Indian boys. *Very brave.*"

"Ya-hey," Victor said. "That's a good one. I wish I could be a warrior."

"Me, too," Thomas said.

They went home together in the dark, Thomas on the bike now, Victor on foot. They walked through shadows and light from streetlamps.

"We've come a long ways," Thomas said. "We have outdoor lighting."

"All I need is the stars," Victor said. "And besides, you still think about things too much."

They separated then, each headed for home, both laughing all the way.

Victor sat at his kitchen table. He counted his one hundred dollars again and again. He knew he needed more to make it to Phoenix and back. He knew he needed Thomas Builds-the-Fire. So he put his money in his wallet and opened the front door to find Thomas on the porch.

"Ya-hey, Victor," Thomas said. "I knew you'd call me."

Thomas walked into the living room and sat down on Victor's favorite chair.

"I've got some money saved up," Thomas said. "It's enough to get us down there, but you have to get us back."

"I've got this hundred dollars," Victor said. "And my dad had a savings account I'm going to claim."

"How much in your dad's account?"

"Enough. A few hundred."

"Sounds good. When we leaving?"

*   *   *

When they were fifteen and had long since stopped being friends, Victor and Thomas got into a fistfight. That is, Victor was really drunk and beat Thomas up for no reason at all. All the other Indian boys stood around and watched it happen. Junior was there and so were Lester, Seymour, and a lot of others. The beating might have gone on until Thomas was dead if Norma Many Horses hadn't come along and stopped it.

"Hey, you boys," Norma yelled and jumped out of her car. "Leave him alone."

If it had been someone else, even another man, the Indian boys would've just ignored the warnings. But Norma was a warrior. She was powerful. She could have picked up any two of the boys and smashed their skulls together. But worse than that, she would have dragged them all over to some tipi and made them listen to some elder tell a dusty old story.

The Indian boys scattered, and Norma walked over to Thomas and picked him up.

"Hey, little man, are you okay?" she asked.

Thomas gave her a thumbs up.

"Why they always picking on you?"

Thomas shook his head, closed his eyes, but no stories came to him, no words or music. He just wanted to go home, to lie in his bed and let his dreams tell his stories for him.

Thomas Builds-the-Fire and Victor sat next to each other in the airplane, coach section. A tiny white woman had the window seat. She was busy twisting her body into pretzels. She was flexible.

"I have to ask," Thomas said, and Victor closed his eyes in embarrassment.

"Don't," Victor said.

"Excuse me, miss," Thomas asked. "Are you a gymnast or something?"

"There's no something about it," she said. "I was first alternate on the 1980 Olympic team."

"Really?" Thomas asked.

"Really."

"I mean, you used to be a world-class athlete?" Thomas asked.

"My husband still thinks I am."

Thomas Builds-the-Fire smiled. She was a mental gymnast, too. She pulled her leg straight up against her body so that she could've kissed her kneecap.

"I wish I could do that," Thomas said.

Victor was ready to jump out of the plane. Thomas, that crazy Indian storyteller with ratty old braids and broken teeth, was flirting with a beautiful Olympic gymnast. Nobody back home on the reservation would ever believe it.

"Well," the gymnast said. "It's easy. Try it."

Thomas grabbed at his leg and tried to pull it up into the same position as the gymnast. He couldn't even come close, which made Victor and the gymnast laugh.

"Hey," she asked. "You two are Indian, right?"

"Full-blood," Victor said.

"Not me," Thomas said. "I'm half magician on my mother's side and half clown on my father's."

They all laughed.

"What are your names?" she asked.

"Victor and Thomas."

"Mine is Cathy. Pleased to meet you all."

The three of them talked for the duration of the flight. Cathy the gymnast complained about the government, how they screwed the 1980 Olympic team by boycotting.

"Sounds like you all got a lot in common with Indians," Thomas said.

Nobody laughed.

After the plane landed in Phoenix and they had all found their way to the terminal, Cathy the gymnast smiled and waved good-bye.

"She was really nice," Thomas said.

"Yeah, but everybody talks to everybody on airplanes," Victor said. "It's too bad we can't always be that way."

"You always used to tell me I think too much," Thomas said. "Now it sounds like you do."

"Maybe I caught it from you."

"Yeah."

Thomas and Victor rode in a taxi to the trailer where Victor's father died.

"Listen," Victor said as they stopped in front of the trailer. "I never told you I was sorry for beating you up that time."

"Oh, it was nothing. We were just kids and you were drunk."

"Yeah, but I'm still sorry."

"That's all right."

Victor paid for the taxi and the two of them stood in the hot Phoenix summer. They could smell the trailer.

"This ain't going to be nice," Victor said. "You don't have to go in."

"You're going to need help."

Victor walked to the front door and opened it. The stink rolled out and made them both gag. Victor's father had lain in that trailer for a week in hundred-degree temperatures before anyone found him. And the only reason anyone found him was because of the smell. They needed dental records to identify him. That's exactly what the coroner said. They needed dental records.

"Oh, man," Victor said. "I don't know if I can do this."

"Well, then don't."

"But there might be something valuable in there."

"I thought his money was in the bank."

"It is. I was talking about pictures and letters and stuff like that."

"Oh," Thomas said as he held his breath and followed Victor into the trailer.

When Victor was twelve, he stepped into an underground wasp nest. His foot was caught in the hole, and no matter how hard he struggled, Victor couldn't pull free. He might have died there, stung a thousand times, if Thomas Builds-the-Fire had not come by.

"Run," Thomas yelled and pulled Victor's foot from the hole. They ran then, hard as they ever had, faster than Billy Mills, faster than Jim Thorpe, faster than the wasps could fly.

Victor and Thomas ran until they couldn't breathe, ran until it was cold and dark outside, ran until they were lost and it took hours to find their way home. All the way back, Victor counted his stings.

"Seven," Victor said. "My lucky number."

* * *

Victor didn't find much to keep in the trailer. Only a photo album and a stereo. Everything else had that smell stuck in it or was useless anyway.

"I guess this is all," Victor said. "It ain't much."

"Better than nothing," Thomas said.

"Yeah, and I do have the pickup."

"Yeah," Thomas said. "It's in good shape."

"Dad was good about that stuff."

"Yeah, I remember your dad."

"Really?" Victor asked. "What do you remember?"

Thomas Builds-the-Fire closed his eyes and told this story: "I remember when I had this dream that told me to go to Spokane, to stand by the Falls in the middle of the city and wait for a sign. I knew I had to go there but I didn't have a car. Didn't have a license. I was only thirteen. So I walked all the way, took me all day, and I finally made it to the Falls. I stood there for an hour waiting. Then your dad came walking up. *What the hell are you doing here?* he asked me. I said, *Waiting for a vision.* Then your father said, *All you're going to get here is mugged.* So he drove me over to Denny's, bought me dinner, and then drove me home to the reservation. For a long time I was mad because I thought my dreams had lied to me. But they didn't. Your dad was my vision. *Take care of each other* is what my dreams were saying. *Take care of each other.*"

Victor was quiet for a long time. He searched his mind for memories of his father, found the good ones, found a few bad ones, added it all up, and smiled.

"My father never told me about finding you in Spokane," Victor said.

"He said he wouldn't tell anybody. Didn't want me to get in trouble. But he said I had to watch out for you as part of the deal."

"Really?"

"Really. Your father said you would need the help. He was right."

"That's why you came down here with me, isn't it?" Victor asked.

"I came because of your father."

Victor and Thomas climbed into the pickup, drove over to the bank, and claimed the three hundred dollars in the savings account.

Thomas Builds-the-Fire could fly.

Once, he jumped off the roof of the tribal school and flapped his arms like a crazy eagle. And he flew. For a second, he hovered, suspended above all the other Indian boys who were too smart or too scared to jump.

"He's flying," Junior yelled, and Seymour was busy looking for the trick wires or mirrors. But it was real. As real as the dirt when Thomas lost altitude and crashed to the ground.

He broke his arm in two places.

"He broke his wing," Victor chanted, and the other Indian boys joined in, made it a tribal song.

"He broke his wing, he broke his wing, he broke his wing," all the Indian boys chanted as they ran off, flapping their wings, wishing they could fly, too. They hated Thomas for his courage, his brief moment as a bird. Everybody has dreams about flying. Thomas flew.

One of his dreams came true for just a second, just enough to make it real.

Victor's father, his ashes, fit in one wooden box with enough left over to fill a cardboard box.

"He always was a big man," Thomas said.

Victor carried part of his father and Thomas carried the rest out to the pickup. They set him down carefully behind the seats, put a cowboy hat on the wooden box and a Dodgers cap on the cardboard box. That's the way it was supposed to be.

"Ready to head back home," Victor asked.

"It's going to be a long drive."

"Yeah, take a couple days, maybe."

"We can take turns," Thomas said.

"Okay," Victor said, but they didn't take turns. Victor drove for sixteen hours straight north, made it halfway up Nevada toward home before he finally pulled over.

"Hey, Thomas," Victor said. "You got to drive for a while."

"Okay."

Thomas Builds-the-Fire slid behind the wheel and started off down the road. All through Nevada, Thomas and Victor had been amazed at the lack of animal life, at the absence of water, of movement.

"Where is everything?" Victor had asked more than once.

Now when Thomas was finally driving they saw the first animal, maybe the only animal in Nevada. It was a long-eared jackrabbit.

"Look," Victor yelled. "It's alive."

Thomas and Victor were busy congratulating themselves on their discovery when the jackrabbit darted out into the road and under the wheels of the pickup.

"Stop the goddamn car," Victor yelled, and Thomas did stop, backed the pickup to the dead jackrabbit.

"Oh, man, he's dead," Victor said as he looked at the squashed animal.

"Really dead."

"The only thing alive in this whole state and we just killed it."

"I don't know," Thomas said. "I think it was suicide."

Victor looked around the desert, sniffed the air, felt the emptiness and loneliness, and nodded his head.

"Yeah," Victor said. "It had to be suicide."

"I can't believe this," Thomas said. "You drive for a thousand miles and there ain't even any bugs smashed on the windshield. I drive for ten seconds and kill the only living thing in Nevada."

"Yeah," Victor said. "Maybe I should drive."

"Maybe you should."

Thomas Builds-the-Fire walked through the corridors of the tribal school by himself. Nobody wanted to be anywhere near him because of all those stories. Story after story.

Thomas closed his eyes and this story came to him: "We are all given one thing by which our lives are measured, one determination. Mine are the stories which can change or not change the world. It doesn't matter which as long as I continue to tell the stories. My father, he died on Okinawa in World War II, died fighting for this country, which had tried to kill him for years. My mother, she died giving birth to me, died while I was still inside her. She pushed me out into the world with her last breath. I have no brothers or sisters. I have only my stories which came to me before I even had the words to speak. I learned a thousand stories before I took my first thousand steps. They are all I have. It's all I can do."

Thomas Builds-the-Fire told his stories to all those who would stop and listen. He kept telling them long after people had stopped listening.

Victor and Thomas made it back to the reservation just as the sun was rising. It was the beginning of a new day on earth, but the same old shit on the reservation.

"Good morning," Thomas said.

"Good morning."

The tribe was waking up, ready for work, eating breakfast, reading the newspaper, just like everybody else does. Willene LeBret was out in her garden wearing a bathrobe. She waved when Thomas and Victor drove by.

"Crazy Indians made it," she said to herself and went back to her roses.

Victor stopped the pickup in front of Thomas Builds-the-Fire's HUD house. They both yawned, stretched a little, shook dust from their bodies.

"I'm tired," Victor said.

"Of everything," Thomas added.

They both searched for words to end the journey. Victor

needed to thank Thomas for his help, for the money, and make the promise to pay it all back.

"Don't worry about the money," Thomas said. "It don't make any difference anyhow."

"Probably not, enit?"

"Nope."

Victor knew that Thomas would remain the crazy storyteller who talked to dogs and cars, who listened to the wind and pine trees. Victor knew that he couldn't really be friends with Thomas, even after all that had happened. It was cruel but it was real. As real as the ashes, as Victor's father, sitting behind the seats.

"I know how it is," Thomas said. "I know you ain't going to treat me any better than you did before. I know your friends would give you too much shit about it."

Victor was ashamed of himself. Whatever happened to the tribal ties, the sense of community? The only real thing he shared with anybody was a bottle and broken dreams. He owed Thomas something, anything.

"Listen," Victor said and handed Thomas the cardboard box which contained half of his father. "I want you to have this."

Thomas took the ashes and smiled, closed his eyes, and told this story: "I'm going to travel to Spokane Falls one last time and toss these ashes into the water. And your father will rise like a salmon, leap over the bridge, over me, and find his way home. It will be beautiful. His teeth will shine like silver, like a rainbow. He will rise, Victor, he will rise."

Victor smiled.

"I was planning on doing the same thing with my half,"

Victor said. "But I didn't imagine my father looking anything like a salmon. I thought it'd be like cleaning the attic or something. Like letting things go after they've stopped having any use."

"Nothing stops, cousin," Thomas said. "Nothing stops."

Thomas Builds-the-Fire got out of the pickup and walked up his driveway. Victor started the pickup and began the drive home.

"Wait," Thomas yelled suddenly from his porch. "I just got to ask one favor."

Victor stopped the pickup, leaned out the window, and shouted back. "What do you want?"

"Just one time when I'm telling a story somewhere, why don't you stop and listen?" Thomas asked.

"Just once?"

"Just once."

Victor waved his arms to let Thomas know that the deal was good. It was a fair trade, and that was all Victor had ever wanted from his whole life. So Victor drove his father's pickup toward home while Thomas went into his house, closed the door behind him, and heard a new story come to him in the silence afterwards.

THE FUN HOUSE

In the trailer by Tshimikain Creek where my cousins
and I used to go crazy in the mud, my aunt waited.
She sewed to pass the time, made beautiful buckskin outfits that
no one could afford, and once she made a full-length beaded
dress that was too heavy for anyone to wear.

"It's just like the sword in the stone," she said. "When
a woman comes along who can carry the weight of this dress on
her back, then we'll have found the one who will save us all."

One morning she sewed while her son and husband
watched television. It was so quiet that when her son released a

tremendous fart, a mouse, startled from his hiding place beneath my aunt's sewing chair, ran straight up her pant leg.

She pulled her body into the air, reached down her pants, unbuttoned them, tried to pull them off, but they stuck around the hips.

"Jesus, Jesus," she cried while her husband and son rolled with laughter on the floor.

"Get it out, get it out," she yelled some more while her husband ran over and smacked her legs in an effort to smash the mouse dead.

"Not that way," she cried again and again.

All the noise and laughter and tears frightened the mouse even more, and he ran down my aunt's pant leg, out the door and into the fields.

In the aftermath, my aunt hiked her pants back up and cursed her son and husband.

"Why didn't you help me?" she asked.

Her son couldn't stop laughing.

"I bet when that mouse ran up your pant leg, he was thinking, *What in the hell kind of mousetraps do they got now?*" her husband said.

"Yeah," her son agreed. "When he got up there, he probably said to himself, *That's the ugliest mousetrap I've ever seen!*"

"Stop it, you two," she yelled. "Haven't you got any sense left?"

"Calm down," my uncle said. "We're only teasing you."

"You're just a couple of ungrateful shits," my aunt said. "Where would you be if I didn't cook, if my fry bread didn't fill your stomachs every damn night?"

"Momma," her son said. "I didn't mean it."

"Yeah," she said. "And I didn't mean to give birth to you. Look at you. Thirty years old and no job except getting drunk. What good are you?"

"That's enough," her husband yelled.

"It's never enough," my aunt said and walked outside, stood in the sun, and searched the sky for predators of any variety. She hoped some falcon or owl would find the mouse and she hoped some pterodactyl would grab her husband and son.

Bird feed, she thought. *They'd make good bird feed.*

In the dark my aunt and her husband were dancing. Thirty years ago and they two-stepped in an Indian cowboy bar. So many Indians in one place and it was beautiful then. All they needed to survive was the drive home after closing time.

"Hey, Nezzy," a voice cried out to my aunt. "You still stepping on toes?"

My aunt smiled and laughed. She was a beautiful dancer, had given lessons at the Arthur Murray Dance Studio to pay her way through community college. She had also danced topless in a Seattle bar to put food in her child's stomach.

There are all kinds of dancing.

"Do you love me?" my aunt asked her husband.

He smiled. He held her closer, tighter. They kept dancing.

After closing time, they drove home on the back roads.

"Be careful," my aunt told her husband. "You drank too much tonight."

He smiled. He put his foot to the fire wall and the pickup

staggered down the dirt road, went on two wheels on a sharp corner, flipped, and slid into the ditch.

My aunt crawled out of the wreck, face full of blood, and sat on the roadside. Her husband had been thrown out of the pickup and lay completely still in the middle of the road.

"Dead? Knocked out? Passed out?" my aunt asked herself.

After a while, another car arrived and stopped. They wrapped an old shirt around my aunt's head and loaded her husband into the backseat.

"Is he dead?" my aunt asked.

"Nah, he'll be all right."

They drove that way to the tribal hospital. My aunt bled into the shirt; her husband slept through his slight concussion. They kept him overnight for observation, and my aunt slept on a cot beside his bed. She left the television on with the volume turned off.

At sunrise my aunt shook her husband awake.

"What?" he asked, completely surprised. "Where am I?"

"In the hospital."

"Again?"

"Yeah, again."

Thirty years later and they still hadn't paid the bill for services rendered.

My aunt walked down her dirt road until she was dizzy. She walked until she stood on the bank of Tshimikain Creek. The water was brown, smelled a little of dead animal and uranium. My cousins and I dove into these waters years ago to pull colored stones from the muddy bottom and collect them in piles beside the creek. My aunt stood beside one of those ordinary monuments to childhood and smiled a little, cried a little.

"One dumb mouse tears apart the whole damn house," she said. Then she stripped off her clothes, kept her shoes on for safety, and dove naked into the creek. She splashed around, screamed in joy as she waded through. She couldn't swim but the creek was shallow, only just past her hips. When she sat down the surface rested just below her chin, so whenever she moved she swallowed a mouthful of water.

"I'll probably get sick," she said and laughed just as her husband and son arrived at the creek, out of breath.

"What the hell are you doing?" her husband asked.

"Swimming."

"But you don't know how to swim."

"I do now."

"Get out of there before you drown," her husband said. "And get some clothes on."

"I'm not coming out until I want to," my aunt said, and she floated up on her back for the first time.

"You can't do that," her son yelled now. "What if somebody sees you?"

"I don't care," my aunt said. "They can all go to hell, and you two can drive the buses that get them there."

Her husband and son threw their hands up in surrender, walked away.

"And cook your own damn dinner," my aunt yelled at their backs.

She floated on the water like that for hours, until her

skin wrinkled and her ears filled with water. She kept her eyes closed and could barely hear when her husband and son came back every so often to plead with her.

"One dumb mouse tore apart the whole damn house. One dumb mouse tore apart the whole damn house," she chanted at them, sang it like a nursery rhyme, like a reservation Mother Goose.

The delivery room was a madhouse, a fun house. The Indian Health Service doctor kept shouting at the nurses.

"Goddamn it," he yelled. "I've never done this before. You've got to help me."

My aunt was conscious, too far into delivery for drugs, and she was screaming a little bit louder than the doctor.

"Shit, shit, fuck," she yelled and grabbed onto the nurses, the doctors, kicked at her stirrups. "It hurts, it hurts, it hurts!"

Her son slid out of her then and nearly slipped through the doctor's hands. The doctor caught him by an ankle and held on tightly.

"It's a boy," he said. "Finally."

A nurse took the baby, held it upside down as she cleared his mouth, wiped his body almost clean. My aunt took her upside-down son with only one question: *Will he love to eat potatoes?*

While my aunt held her baby close to her chest, the doctor tied her tubes, with the permission slip my aunt signed because the hospital administrator lied and said it proved her Indian status for the BIA.

"What are you going to name it?" a nurse asked my aunt.

"Potatoes," she said. "Or maybe Albert."

When the sun went down and the night got too cold, my aunt finally surrendered the water of Tshimikain Creek, put clothes on her damp and tired body, and walked up her road toward home. She looked at the bright lights shining in the windows, listened to the dogs bark stupidly, and knew that things had to change.

She walked into the house, didn't say a word to her stunned husband and son, and pulled that heaviest of beaded dresses over her head. Her knees buckled and she almost fell from the weight; then she did fall.

"No," she said to her husband and son as they rose to help her.

She stood, weakly. But she had the strength to take the first step, then another quick one. She heard drums, she heard singing, she danced.

Dancing that way, she knew things were beginning to change.

ALL I WANTED TO DO
WAS DANCE

V ictor was dancing with a Lakota woman in a Montana bar. He had no idea why he was there; he couldn't even remember how he arrived. All he knew was that he was dancing with the one hundredth Indian woman in the one hundred dancing days since the white woman he loved had left him. This dancing was his compensation, his confession, largest sin, and penance.

"You're beautiful," he said to the Lakota woman.

"And you're drunk," she said. But she was beautiful, with hair and eyes so dark and long. He imagined she was a reservation eclipse. Full. He needed special glasses to look at her; he could barely survive her reflection.

"You're a constellation," he said.

"And you're really drunk," she said.

Then she was gone and he was laughing, dancing through the bar all by himself. He wanted to sing but he couldn't think of any lyrics. He was drunk, bruised by whiskey, brutal. His hair was electricity.

"I started World War I," he shouted. "I shot Lincoln."

He was underwater drunk, staring up at the faces of his past. He recognized Neil Armstrong and Christopher Columbus, his mother and father, James Dean, Sal Mineo, Natalie Wood. He staggered, fell against other dancers, found himself in the backseat of a Grasshopper as it traveled uneasily down reservation dirt roads.

"Where are we?" he asked the Flathead driver with insane braids.

"Heading back to Arlee, cousin. You said you wanted a ride."

"Shit, all I wanted to do was dance."

By the river. She was standing by the river. She was dancing without moving. By the river. She wasn't beautiful exactly; she was like a shimmer in the distance. She was so white his reservation eyes suffered.

"Hey," Victor asked. "Haven't you ever heard of Custer?"

"Have you ever heard of Crazy Horse?" she asked him.

In his memory she was all kinds of colors, but the only one that really mattered was white. Then she was gone, and absence has no color. Sometimes he looked in the mirror, rubbed his face, pulled at his eyelids and skin. He combed his hair into braids and forgave himself. At night his legs ached and he reached down under the covers and touched his thighs, flexed muscles. He opened his eyes but all he could see in the dark was the digital clock on the milk carton beside the bed. It was late, early in the morning. He kept his eyes open until they grew accustomed to the dark, until he could see vague images of the bedroom. Then he looked at the clock again. Fifteen minutes had passed and it was closer to sunrise and he still hadn't slept at all.

He measured insomnia by minutes. *Ten minutes*, he told himself. *I'll be asleep in ten minutes. If not, I'll get up and turn on the light. Read a book maybe.*

Ten minutes passed and he made more promises. *It's hopeless. If I'm not asleep in half an hour, I'll get up and make some breakfast. I'll watch the sunrise. Vacuum.*

When dawn finally arrived, he lay awake for a few minutes, ran his tongue over his teeth. He reached out and touched the other half of his bed. No one was supposed to be there; he just stretched his arms. Then he rose quickly, showered, shaved, and sat at the kitchen table with his coffee and newspaper. He read headlines, a few Help Wanted ads, and circled one with a pencil.

"Good morning," he said aloud, then louder. "Good morning."

* * *

"People change," she told Victor. He watched her face as she spoke and watched her hands when she touched his arm.

"I wouldn't know about that," he said. Her hands were white and small. He remembered how white and small they looked against his brown skin as they lay together, wrapped in sheets. She fell asleep easily and he watched her, listened to her breathing, until his breath fell into the same rhythm, until he slept.

"I miss watching you sleep," he said.

"Listen, things are just crazy right now. I went to a party the other night and someone had some cocaine, you know? It was there and I liked it."

"You mean you snorted it?"

"No, no. I just liked it being there. I danced, too. There was music, and people were dancing out by the pool. So I danced."

He stared at her then. She smiled and touched her face, brushed hair away from her eyes.

"God," she said. "I could really get addicted to cocaine, you know? I could really like it."

Victor sipped his coffee carefully even though it was lukewarm. He stared out over the cup, through the window into the sun rising. He felt dizzy and didn't stand up for fear of falling. His eyes were heavy, ached.

"Today," he said to his coffee, "I'm going to run."

He imagined pulling on a pair of shorts and his tennis shoes, stretching his muscles on the back porch before he set out into the early morning. Two, maybe three miles out and then back to the house. A few sit-ups, push-ups, to cool down and a piece of dry toast to settle his stomach. Instead, he finished his coffee and switched on the television, flipped through a few stations before he found a face he liked. A pretty blond woman was reading the local news, but he turned the volume all the way down, watched her mouth working silently.

Soon she was replaced by other faces, tired reporters with windblown hair, a forest fire, another war. It was all the same. Once, he owned a black-and-white television. He thought everything was much clearer then. Color complicated even the smallest events. A commercial for a new candy bar was so bright, so layered, he ran to the bathroom and threw up.

Still, he drank his coffee straight today. In other yesterdays he poured vodka into his cup before the coffee was finished brewing.

"Shit," he said aloud. "Nothing more hopeless than a sober Indian."

Victor was fancydancing. Eight, maybe nine years old and he was fancydancing in the same outfit his father wore as a child. The feathers were genetic; the fringe was passed down like the curve of his face.

Drums.

He looked into the crowd for approval, saw his mother and father. He waved and they waved back. Smiles and Indian teeth. They were both drunk. Everything familiar and welcome. Everything beautiful.

Drums.

After the dance, back at camp, he ate fry bread with too

much butter and drank a Pepsi just pulled from the cooler. The Pepsi was partly frozen and the little pieces of ice hurt his teeth.

"Did you see Junior dancing?" his mother asked everyone in camp. She was loud, drunk, staggered.

They all nodded heads in agreement; this other kind of dancing was nothing new. His father passed out beneath the picnic table, and after a while his mother crawled under, wrapped her arms around her husband, and passed out with him. Of course, they were in love.

Drums.

Victor was drunk again.

A night in the wooden-floor bar and she wanted to dance, but he wanted to drink and ease that tug in his throat and gut.

"Come on, you've had enough," she said.

"Just one more beer, sweetheart, and then we'll go home."

It happened that way. He thought one more beer could save the world. One more beer and every chair would be comfortable. One more beer and the light bulb in the bathroom would never burn out. One more beer and he would love her forever. One more beer and he would sign any treaty for her.

At home, in the dark, they fought and kicked at sheets, at each other. She waited for him to pass out. He drank so much but he would never pass out. He cried.

"Goddamn it," he said. "I hate the fucking world."

"Go to sleep."

He closed his eyes; he played the stereo at full volume. He punched the walls but never hard enough to hurt himself.

"Nothing works. Nothing works."

Mornings after, he would pretend sleep while she dressed, left for work and her own home. Mornings after, she paused at the door before leaving, asked herself if this was for good.

One morning, it was.

Sometimes Victor worked.

He drove a garbage truck for the BIA; he cooked hamburgers at the Tribal Cafe. On payday, his wallet stuffed with money, he would stand in front of the beer cooler in the Trading Post.

"How long has he been standing there?" Phyllis asked Seymour.

"Some say he's been there for hours. That woman over there with the music case says Victor has been standing there his whole life. I think he's been there for five hundred years."

Once, Victor bought a case of Coors Light and drove for miles with the bottles beside him on the seat. He would open one, touch the cold glass to his lips, and feel his heart stagger. But he could not drink, and one by one he tossed twenty-four full bottles out the window.

The small explosions, their shattering, was the way he measured time.

* * *

Victor watched the morning arrive and leave. His hands were cold. He pressed them against the window glass and waited for some warmth to translate. He'd been back home on the reservation for one hundred days after being lost in the desert for forty years. But he wasn't going to save anyone. Maybe not even himself.

He opened his front door to watch the world revolving. He walked onto his front porch and felt the cold air. Tomorrow he would run. He would be somebody's hero. Tomorrow.

He counted his coins. Enough for a bottle of Annie Green Springs Wine in the Trading Post. He walked down the hill and into the store, grabbed the bottle without hesitation, paid for it with nickels and pennies, and walked into the parking lot. Victor pulled the wine from its paper bag, cracked the seal, and twisted the cap off.

Jesus, he wanted to drink so much his blood could make the entire tribe numb.

"Hey, cousin, you got to let it breathe."

An Indian stranger jumped from a pickup, walked over to Victor, and smiled.

"What did you say?" Victor asked him.

"I said you got to let it breathe."

Victor looked at his open bottle, offered it to the stranger in an intertribal gesture.

"You want the first drink, cousin?"

"Don't mind if I do."

The stranger drank long and hard, his throat working like gears. When he was done, he wiped the bottle clean and handed it back to Victor.

"Listen up," the stranger said. "Today is my birthday."

"How old are you?"

"Old enough."

And they laughed.

Victor looked at the bottle again and offered it again to the stranger in a personal gesture.

"Have a birthday drink."

"Shit, you're a generous drunk, enit?"

"Generous enough."

And they laughed.

The Indian stranger drank half the bottle with one swallow. He smiled when he handed the wine back to Victor.

"What tribe are you, cousin?" Victor asked him.

"Cherokee."

"Really? Shit, I've never met a real Cherokee."

"Neither have I."

And they laughed.

Victor looked at the bottle for a third time. He handed it back to the Indian stranger.

"Keep it," he said. "You deserve it more."

"Thanks, cousin. My throat is dry, you know?"

"Yeah, I know."

Victor touched the Indian stranger's hand, smiled hard at him, and walked away. He looked at the sun to determine the time and then checked his watch to be sure.

"Hey, cousin," the Indian stranger yelled. "You know how to tell the difference between a real Indian and a fake Indian?"

"How?"

"The real Indian got blisters on his feet. The fake Indian got blisters on his ass."

And they laughed. And Victor kept laughing as he walked. And he was walking down this road and tomorrow maybe he would be walking down another road and maybe tomorrow he would be dancing. Victor might be dancing.

Yes, Victor would be dancing.

THE TRIAL OF THOMAS
BUILDS-THE-FIRE

Someone must have been telling lies about Joseph K., for without
having done anything wrong he was arrested one fine morning.

—Franz Kafka

T homas Builds-the-Fire waited alone in the Spokane
tribal holding cell while BIA officials discussed his
future, the immediate present, and of course, his past.

"Builds-the-Fire has a history of this kind of behavior,"
a man in a BIA suit said to the others. "A storytelling fetish
accompanied by an extreme need to tell the truth. Dangerous."

Thomas was in the holding cell because he had once held
the reservation postmaster hostage for eight hours with the idea
of a gun and had also threatened to make significant changes
in the tribal vision. But that crisis was resolved years ago as

Thomas surrendered voluntarily and agreed to remain silent. In fact, Thomas had not spoken in nearly twenty years. All his stories remained internal; he would not even send letters or Christmas cards.

But recently Thomas had begun to make small noises, form syllables that contained more emotion and meaning than entire sentences constructed by the BIA. A noise that sounded something like *rain* had given Esther courage enough to leave her husband, tribal chairman David WalksAlong, who had been tribal police chief at the time of Thomas Builds-the-Fire's original crime. WalksAlong walked along with BIA policy so willingly that he took to calling his wife *a savage in polyester pants*. She packed her bags the day after she listened to Thomas speak; Thomas was arrested the day after Esther left.

Now Thomas sat quietly in his cell, counting cockroaches and silverfish. He couldn't sleep, he didn't feel like eating. Often he closed his eyes and stories came to him quickly, but he would not speak. He nodded and laughed if the story was funny; cried a little when the stories were sad; pounded his fists against his mattress when the stories angered him.

"Well, the traveling judge is coming in tomorrow," one guy in a BIA suit said to the others. "What charges should we bring him up on?"

"Inciting a riot? Kidnapping? Extortion? Maybe murder?" another guy in a BIA suit asked, and the others laughed.

"Well," they all agreed. "It has to be a felony charge. We don't need his kind around here anymore."

Later that night, Thomas lay awake and counted stars through the bars in his window. He was guilty, he knew that. All that was variable on any reservation was how the convicted would be punished.

The following report is adapted from the original court transcript.

"Mr. Builds-the-Fire," the judge said to Thomas. "Before we begin this trial, the court must be certain that you understand the charges against you."

Thomas, who wore his best ribbon shirt and decided to represent himself, stood and spoke a complete sentence for the first time in two decades.

"Your Honor," he said. "I don't believe that the exact nature of any charges against me have been revealed, let alone detailed."

There was a hush in the crowd, followed by exclamations of joy, sadness, etc. Eve Ford, the former reservation postmaster held hostage by Thomas years earlier, sat quietly in the back row and thought to herself, *He hasn't done anything wrong.*

"Well, Mr. Builds-the-Fire," the judge said. "I can only infer by your sudden willingness to communicate that you do in fact understand the purpose of this trial."

"That's not true."

"Are you accusing this court of dishonesty, Mr. Builds-the-Fire?"

Thomas sat down, to regain his silence for a few moments.

"Well, Mr. Builds-the-Fire, we're going to dispense with

opening remarks and proceed to testimony. Are you ready to call your first witness?''

"Yes, I am, Your Honor. I call myself as first and only witness to all the crimes I'm accused of and, additionally, to bring attention to all the mitigating circumstances."

"Whatever," the judge said. "Raise your right hand and promise me you'll tell the whole truth and nothing but the truth."

"Honesty is all I have left," Thomas said.

Thomas Builds-the-Fire sat in the witness stand, closed his eyes, and spoke this story aloud:

"It all started on September 8, 1858. I was a young pony, strong and quick in every movement. I remember this. Still, there was so much to fear on that day when Colonel George Wright took me and 799 of my brothers captive. Imagine, 800 beautiful ponies stolen at once. It was the worst kind of war crime. But Colonel Wright thought we were too many to transport, that we were all dangerous. In fact, I still carry his letter of that day which justified the coming slaughter":

Dear Sir:

As I reported in my communication of yesterday the capture of 800 horses on the 8th instant, I have now to add that this large band of horses composed the entire wealth of the Spokane chief Til-co-ax. This man has ever been hostile; for the last two years he has been constantly sending his young men into the Walla Walla valley, and stealing horses and cattle from the settlers and from the government. He boldly acknowledged these facts when he met Colonel

Steptoe, in May last. Retributive justice has now over-
taken him; the blow has been severe but well merited.
I found myself embarrassed with these 800 horses. I
could not hazard the experiment of moving with such
a number of animals (many of them very wild) along
with my large train; should a stampede take place, we
might not only lose our captured animals, but many
of our own. Under those circumstances, I determined
to kill them all, save a few in service in the quarter-
master's department and to replace broken-down animals. I deeply regretted killing these poor creatures,
but a dire necessity drove me to it. This work of
slaughter has been going on since 10 o'clock of yesterday, and will not be completed before this evening,
and I shall march for the Coeur d'Alene Mission
tomorrow.

Very respectfully, your obedient servant,
G. WRIGHT, Colonel 9th Infantry, Commanding.

"Somehow I was lucky enough to be spared while hundreds of my brothers and sisters fell together. It was a nightmare
to witness. They were rounded into a corral and then lassoed,
one by one, and dragged out to be shot in the head. This lasted
for hours, and all that dark night mothers cried for their dead
children. The next day, the survivors were rounded into a single
mass and slaughtered by continuous rifle fire."

Thomas opened his eyes and found that most of the
Indians in the courtroom wept and wanted to admit defeat. He
then closed his eyes and continued the story:

"But I was not going to submit without a struggle. I

97

would continue the war. At first I was passive, let one man saddle me and ride for a while. He laughed at the illusion of my weakness. But I suddenly rose up and bucked him off and broke his arm. Another man tried to ride me, but I threw him and so many others, until I was lathered with sweat and blood from their spurs and rifle butts. It was glorious. Finally they gave up, quit, and led me to the back of the train. They could not break me. Some may have wanted to kill me for my arrogance, but others respected my anger, my refusal to admit defeat. I lived that day, even escaped Colonel Wright, and galloped into other histories."

Thomas opened his eyes and saw that the Indians in the courtroom sat up straight, combed their braids gracefully, smiled with Indian abandon.

"Mr. Builds-the-Fire," the judge asked. "Is that the extent of your testimony?"

"Your Honor, if I may continue, there is much more I need to say. There are so many more stories to tell."

The judge looked at Thomas Builds-the-Fire for an instant, decided to let him continue. Thomas closed his eyes, and a new story was raised from the ash of older stories:

"My name was Qualchan and I had been fighting for our people, for our land. It was horrendous, hiding in the dirt at the very mouth of the Spokane River where my fellow warrior, Moses, found me after he escaped from Colonel Wright's camp. *Qualchan,* he said to me. *You must stay away from Wright's camp. He means to hang you.* But Wright had taken my father hostage and threatened to hang him if I did not come in. Wright promised he would treat me fairly. I believed him and went to the colonel's camp and was immediately placed in chains. It was then I saw the hangman's noose and made the fight to escape. My wife also fought beside me with a knife and wounded many soldiers before she was subdued. After I was beaten down, they dragged me to the noose and I was hanged with six other Indians, including Epseal, who had never raised a hand in anger to any white or Indian."

Thomas opened his eyes and swallowed air hard. He could barely breathe and the courtroom grew distant and vague.

"Mr. Builds-the-Fire," the judge asked and brought Thomas back to attention. "What point are you trying to make with this story?"

"Well," Thomas said. "The City of Spokane is now building a golf course named after me, Qualchan, located in that valley where I was hanged."

The courtroom burst into motion and emotion. The judge hammered his gavel against his bench. The bailiff had to restrain Eve Ford, who had made a sudden leap of faith across the room toward Thomas.

"Thomas," she yelled. "We're all listening."

The bailiff had his hands full as Eve slugged him twice and then pushed him to the ground. Eve stomped on the bailiff's big belly until two tribal policemen tackled her, handcuffed her, and led her away.

"Thomas," she yelled. "We hear you."

The judge was red-faced with anger; he almost looked Indian. He pounded his gavel until it broke.

"Order in the court," he shouted. "Order in the fucking court."

The tribal policemen grew in number. Many were Indians that the others had never seen before. The policemen swelled

99

in size and forced the others out of the courtroom. After the court was cleared and order restored, the judge pulled his replacement gavel from beneath his robe and continued the trial.

"Now," the judge said. "We can go about the administration of justice."

"Is that real justice or the idea of justice?" Thomas asked him, and the judge flew back into anger.

"Defense testimony is over," he said. "Mr. Builds-the-Fire, you will now be cross-examined."

Thomas watched the prosecuting attorney approach the witness stand.

"Mr. Builds-the-Fire," he said. "Where were you on May 16, 1858?"

"I was in the vicinity of Rosalia, Washington, along with 799 other warriors, ready to battle with Colonel Steptoe and his soldiers."

"And could you explain exactly what happened there that day?"

Thomas closed his eyes and told this story:

"My name was Wild Coyote and I was just sixteen years old and was frightened because this was to be my first battle. But we were confident because Steptoe's soldiers were so small and weak. They tried to negotiate a peace, but our war chiefs would not settle for anything short of blood. You must understand these were days of violence and continual lies from the white man. Steptoe said he wanted peace between whites and Indians, but he had cannons and had lied before, so we refused to believe him this time. Instead, we attacked at dawn and killed many of their soldiers and lost only a few warriors. The soldiers made a stand on a hilltop and we surrounded them, amazed at their tears and cries. But you must understand they were also very brave. The soldiers fought well, but there were too many Indians for them on that day. Night fell and we retreated a little as we always do during dark. Somehow the surviving soldiers escaped during the night, and many of us were happy for them. They had fought so well that they deserved to live another day."

Thomas opened his eyes and found the prosecuting attorney's long nose just inches from his own.

"Mr. Builds-the-Fire, how many soldiers did you kill that day?"

Thomas closed his eyes and told another story:

"I killed one soldier right out with an arrow to the chest. He fell off his horse and didn't move again. I shot another soldier and he fell off his horse, too, and I ran over to him to take his scalp but he pulled his revolver and shot me through the shoulder. I still have the scar. It hurt so much that I left the soldier and went away to die. I really thought I was going to die, and I suppose the soldier probably died later. So I went and lay down in this tall grass and watched the sky. It was beautiful and I was ready to die. It had been a good fight. I lay there for part of the day and most of the night until one of my friends picked me up and said the soldiers had escaped. My friend tied himself to me and we rode away with the others. That is what happened."

Thomas opened his eyes and faced the prosecuting attorney.

"Mr. Builds-the-Fire, you do admit, willingly, that you murdered two soldiers in cold blood and with premeditation?"

"Yes, I killed those soldiers, but they were good men. I

did it with sad heart and hand. There was no way I could ever smile or laugh again. I'm not sorry we had to fight, but I am sorry those men had to die."

"Mr. Builds-the-Fire, please answer the question. Did you or did you not murder those two soldiers in cold blood and with premeditation?"

"I did."

Article from the Spokesman-Review, *October 7, 19—.*

Builds-the-Fire to Smolder in Prison

WELLPINIT, WASHINGTON—Thomas Builds-the-Fire, the self-proclaimed visionary of the Spokane Tribe, was sentenced today to two concurrent life terms in the Walla Walla State Penitentiary. His many supporters battled with police for over eight hours following the verdict.

U.S. District Judge James Wright asked, "Do you have anything you want to say now, Mr. Builds-the-Fire?" Builds-the-Fire simply shook his head no and was led away by prison officials.

Wright told Builds-the-Fire that the new federal sentencing guidelines "require the imposition of a life sentence for racially motivated murder." There is no possibility for parole, said U.S. Prosecuting Attorney, Adolph D. Jim, an enrolled member of the Yakima Indian Nation.

"The only appeal I have is for justice," Builds-

the-Fire reportedly said as he was transported away
from this story and into the next.

Thomas Builds-the-Fire sat quietly as the bus traveled
down the highway toward Walla Walla State Penitentiary. There
were six other prisoners: four African men, one Chicano, and a
white man from the smallest town in the state.

"I know who you are," the Chicano said to Thomas.
"You're that Indian guy did all the talking."

"Yeah," one of the African men said. "You're that storyteller. Tell us some stories, chief, give us the scoop."

Thomas looked at these five men who shared his skin
color, at the white man who shared this bus which was going to
deliver them into a new kind of reservation, barrio, ghetto,
logging-town tin shack. He then looked out the window, through
the steel grates on the windows, at the freedom just outside the
glass. He saw wheat fields, bodies of water, and bodies of dark-
skinned workers pulling fruit from trees and sweat from thin air.

Thomas closed his eyes and told this story.

DISTANCES

All Indians must dance, everywhere, keep on dancing. Pretty soon in next spring Great Spirit come. He bring back all game of every kind. The game be thick everywhere. All dead Indians come back and live again. Old blind Indian see again and get young and have fine time. When Great Spirit comes this way, then all the Indians go to mountains, high up away from whites. Whites can't hurt Indians then. Then while Indians way up high big flood comes like water and all white people die, get drowned. After that, water go away and then nobody but Indians everywhere and game all kinds thick. Then medicine man tell Indians to send word to all Indians to keep up dancing and the good time will come. Indians who don't dance, who don't believe in this word, will grow little, just about a foot high, and stay that way. Some of them will be turned into wood and burned in fire.

—Wovoka, the Paiute Ghost Dance Messiah

After this happened, after it began, I decided Custer could have, must have, pressed the button, cut down all the trees, opened up holes in the ozone, flooded the earth. Since most of the white men died and most of the Indians lived, I decided only Custer could have done something that backward. Or maybe it was because the Ghost Dance finally worked.

* * *

Last night we burned another house. The Tribal Council has ruled that anything to do with the whites has to be destroyed. Sometimes while we are carrying furniture out of a house to be burned, all of us naked, I have to laugh out loud. I wonder if this is how it looked all those years ago when we savage Indians were slaughtering those helpless settlers. We must have been freezing, buried by cold then, too.

I found a little transistor radio in a closet. It's one of those yellow waterproof radios that children always used to have. I know that most of the electrical circuitry was destroyed, all the batteries dead, all the wires shorted, all the dams burst, but I wonder if this radio still works. It was hidden away in a closet under a pile of old quilts, so maybe it was protected. I was too scared to turn it on, though. What would I hear? Farm reports, sports scores, silence?

There's this woman I love, Tremble Dancer, but she's one of the Urbans. Urbans are the city Indians who survived and made their way out to the reservation after it all fell apart. There must have been over a hundred when they first arrived, but most of them have died since. Now there are only a dozen Urbans left, and they're all sick. The really sick ones look like they are five hundred years old. They look like they have lived forever; they look like they'll die soon.

Tremble Dancer isn't sick yet, but she does have burns and scars all over her legs. When she dances around the fire at night, she shakes from the pain. Once when she fell, I caught her and we looked hard at each other. I thought I could see half of her life, something I could remember, something I could never forget.

The Skins, Indians who lived on the reservation when it happened, can never marry Urbans. The Tribal Council made that rule because of the sickness in the Urbans. One of the original Urbans was pregnant when she arrived on the reservation and gave birth to a monster. The Tribal Council doesn't want that to happen again.

Sometimes I ride my clumsy horse out to Noah Chirapkin's tipi. He's the only Skin I know that has traveled off the reservation since it happened.

"There was no sound," he told me once. "I rode for days and days but there were no cars moving, no planes, no bulldozers, no trees. I walked through a city that was empty, walked from one side to the other, and it took me a second. I just blinked my eyes and the city was gone, behind me. I found a single plant, a black flower, in the shadow of Little Falls Dam. It was forty years before I found another one, growing between the walls of an old house on the coast."

Last night I dreamed about television. I woke up crying.

The weather is changed, changing, becoming new. At night it is cold, so cold that fingers can freeze into a face that is touched. During the day, our sun holds us tight against the ground. All the old people die, choosing to drown in their own water rather than die of thirst. All their bodies are evil, the Tribal Council decided. We burn the bodies on the football field, on the fifty-yard line one week, in an end zone the next. I hear rumors that relatives of the dead might be killed and burned, too. The Tribal Council decided it's a white man's disease in their blood. It's a wristwatch that has fallen between their ribs, slowing, stopping. I'm happy my grandparents and parents died before all of this happened. I'm happy I'm an orphan.

Sometimes Tremble Dancer waits for me at the tree, all we have left. We take off our clothes, loincloth, box dress. We climb the branches of the tree and hold each other, watching for the Tribal Council. Sometimes her skin will flake, fall off, float to the ground. Sometimes I taste parts of her breaking off into my mouth. It is the taste of blood, dust, sap, sun.

"My legs are leaving me," Tremble Dancer told me once. "Then it will be my arms, my eyes, my fingers, the small of my back.

"I am jealous of what you have," she told me, pointing at the parts of my body and telling me what they do.

Last night we burned another house. I saw a painting of Jesus Christ lying on the floor.
He's white. Jesus is white.
While the house was burning, I could see flames, colors,

every color but white. I don't know what it means, don't understand fire, the burns on Tremble Dancer's legs, the ash left to cool after the house has been reduced.

I want to know why Jesus isn't a flame.

Last night I dreamed about television. I woke up crying.

While I lie in my tipi pretending to be asleep under the half-blankets of dog and cat skin, I hear the horses exploding. I hear the screams of children who are taken.

The Others have come from a thousand years ago, their braids gray and broken with age. They have come with arrow, bow, stone ax, large hands.

"Do you remember me?" they sing above the noise, our noise.

"Do you still fear me?" they shout above the singing, our singing.

I run from my tipi across the ground toward the tree, climb the branches to watch the Others. There is one, taller than the clouds, who doesn't ride a pony, who runs across the dust, faster than my memory.

Sometimes they come back. The Others, carrying salmon, water. Once, they took Noah Chirapkin, tied him down to the ground, poured water down his throat until he drowned.

The tallest Other, the giant, took Tremble Dancer away, brought her back with a big belly. She smelled of salt, old blood.

She gave birth, salmon flopped from her, salmon growing larger.

When she died, her hands bled seawater from the palms.

At the Tribal Council meeting last night, Judas WildShoe gave a watch he found to the tribal chairman.

"A white man artifact, a sin," the chairman said, put the watch in his pouch.

I remember watches. They measured time in seconds, minutes, hours. They measured time exactly, coldly. I measure time with my breath, the sound of my hands across my own skin.

I make mistakes.

Last night I held my transistor radio in my hands, gently, as if it were alive. I examined it closely, searching for some flaw, some obvious damage. But there was nothing, no imperfection I could see. If there was something wrong, it was not evident by the smooth, hard plastic of the outside. All the mistakes would be on the inside, where you couldn't see, couldn't reach.

I held that radio and turned it on, turned the volume to maximum, until all I could hear was the in and out, in again, of my breath.

JESUS CHRIST'S HALF-BROTHER IS ALIVE AND WELL ON THE SPOKANE INDIAN RESERVATION

1966

Rosemary MorningDove gave birth to a boy today and seeing as how it was nearly Christmas and she kept telling everyone she was still a virgin even though Frank Many Horses said it was his we all just figured it was an accident. Anyhow she gave birth to him but he came out all blue and they couldn't get him to breathe for a long time but he finally did and Rosemary MorningDove named him ———— which is unpronounceable in Indian and English but it means: *He Who Crawls Silently Through the Grass with a Small Bow and One Bad Arrow Hunting for Enough Deer to Feed the Whole Tribe.*

We just call him James.

1967

Frank Many Horses and Lester FallsApart and I were drinking beers in the Breakaway Bar playing pool and talking stories when we heard the sirens. Indians get all excited when we hear sirens because it means fires and it means they need firefighters to put out the fires and it means we get to be firefighters and it means we get paid to be firefighters. Hell somebody always starts a fire down at the Indian burial grounds and it was about time for the Thirteenth Annual All-Indian Burial Grounds Fire so Frank and Lester and I ran down to the fire station expecting to get hired but we see smoke coming from Commodity Village where all the really poor Indians live so we run down there instead and it was Rosemary MorningDove's house that was on fire. Indians got buckets of water but this fire was way too big and we could hear a baby crying and Frank Many Horses gets all excited even though it's Lillian Many's baby right next to us. But Frank knows James is in the house so he goes running in before any of us can stop him and pretty soon I see Frank leaning out the upstairs window holding James and they're both a little on fire and Frank throws James out the window and I'm running my ass over to catch him before he hits the ground making like a high school football hero again but I miss him just barely slipping through my fingers and James hits the ground hard and I pick him up right away and slap the flames out with my hands all the while expecting James to be dead but he's just looking at me almost normal except the top of his head looks all dented in like a beer can.

He wasn't crying.

1967

I went down to the reservation hospital to see how James and Frank and Rosemary were doing and I got drunk just before I went so I wouldn't be scared of all the white walls and the sound of arms and legs getting sawed off down in the basement. But I heard the screams anyway and they were Indian screams and those can travel forever like all around the world and sometimes from a hundred years ago so I close my ears and hide my eyes and just look down at the clean clean floors. Oh Jesus I'm so drunk I want to pray but I don't and before I can change my mind about coming here Moses MorningDove pulls me aside to tell me Frank and Rosemary have died and since I saved James's life I should be the one who raises him. Moses says it's Indian tradition but somehow since Moses is going on about two hundred years old and still drinking and screwing like he was twenty I figure he's just trying to get out of his grandfatherly duties. I don't really want any of it and I'm sick and the hospital is making me sicker and my heart is shaking and confused like when the nurse wakes you up in the middle of the night to give you a sleeping pill but I know James will end up some Indian kid at a welfare house making baskets and wearing itchy clothes and I'm only twenty myself but I take one look at James all lumpy and potato looking and I look in the mirror and see myself holding him and I take him home.

Tonight the mirror will forgive my face.

1967

All dark tonight and James couldn't sleep and just kept looking at the ceiling so I walk on down to the football field carrying James so we can both watch the stars looking down at the reservation. I put James down on the fifty-yard line and I run and run across the frozen grass wishing there was snow enough to make a trail and let the world know I was there in the morning. Thinking I could spell out my name or James's name or every name I could think of until I stepped on every piece of snow on the field like it was every piece of the world or at least every piece of this reservation that has so many pieces it might just be the world. I want to walk circles around James getting closer and closer to him in a new dance and a better kind of healing which could make James talk and walk before he learns to cry. But he's not crying and he's not walking and he's not talking and I see him sometimes like an old man passed out in the back of a reservation van with shit in his pants and a battered watch in his pocket that always shows the same damn time. So I pick James up from the cold and the grass that waits for spring and the sun to change its world but I can only walk home through the cold with another future on my back and James's future tucked in my pocket like an empty wallet or a newspaper that feeds the fire and never gets read.

Sometimes all of this is home.

1968

The world changing the world changing the world. I don't watch the TV anymore since it exploded and left a hole in the wall. The woodpile don't dream of me no more. It sits there by the ax and they talk about the cold that waits in corners and surprises you on a warm almost spring day. Today I stood at the window for hours and then I took the basketball from inside the wood stove and shot baskets at the hoop nailed to a pine tree in the yard. I shot and shot until the cold meant I was protected because my skin was too warm to feel any of it. I shot and shot until my fingertips bled and my feet ached and my hair stuck to the skin of my bare back. James waited by the porch with his hands in the dirt and his feet stuck into leather shoes I found in the dump under a washing machine. I can't believe the details I am forced to remember with each day that James comes closer to talking. I change his clothes and his dirty pants and I wash his face and the crevices of his little body until he shines like a new check.

This is my religion.

1968

Seems like the cold would never go away and winter would be like the bottom of my feet but then it is gone in one night and in its place comes the sun so large and laughable. James sitting up in his chair so young and he won't talk and the doctors at the Indian clinic say it's way too early for him to be talking anyhow but I see in his eyes something and I see in his eyes a voice and I see in his eyes a whole new set of words. It ain't Indian or English and it ain't cash register and it ain't traffic light or speed bump and it ain't window or door. Late one day James and I watch the sun fly across the sky like a basketball on fire until it falls down completely and lands in Benjamin Lake with a splash and shakes the ground and even wakes up Lester Falls-Apart who thought it was his father come back to slap his face again.

Summer coming like a car from down the highway.

1968

James must know how to cry because he hasn't cried yet and I know he's waiting for that one moment to cry like it was five hundred years of tears. He ain't walked anywhere and there are no blisters on his soles but there are dreams worn clean into his rib cage and it shakes and shakes with each breath and I see he's trying to talk when he grabs at the air behind his head or stares up at the sky so hard. All of this temperature rising hot and I set James down in the shade by the basketball court and I play and I play until the sweat of my body makes it rain everywhere on the reservation. I play and I play until the music of my shoes against pavement sounds like every drum. Then I'm home alone and I watch the cockroaches live their complicated lives.

I hold James with one arm and my basketball with the other arm and I hold everything else inside my whole body.

1969

I take James to the Indian clinic because he ain't crying yet and because all he does sometimes is stare and stare and sometimes he'll wrap his arms around the stray dogs and let them carry him around the yard. He's strong enough to hold his body off the ground but he ain't strong enough to lift his tongue from the bottom of his mouth to use the words for love or anger or hunger or good morning. Maybe he's only a few years old but he's got eyes that are ancient and old and dark like a castle or a lake where the turtles go to die and sometimes even to live. Maybe he's going to howl out the words when I least expect it or want it and he'll yell out a cuss word in church or a prayer in the middle of a grocery store. Today I moved through town and walked and walked past the people who hadn't seen me in so long maybe for months and they asked questions about me and James and no one bothered to knock on the door and look for the answers. It's just me and James walking and walking except he's on my back and his eyes are looking past the people who are looking past us for the coyote of our soul and the wolverine of our heart and the crazy crazy man that touches every Indian who spends too much time alone. I stand in the Trading Post touching the canned goods and hoping for a vision of all the miles until Seymour comes in with a twenty-dollar bill and buys a couple cases of beer and we drink and drink all night long. James gets handed from woman to woman and from man to man and a few children hold this child of mine who doesn't cry or recognize the human being in his own body. All the drunks happy to see me drunk again and back from the wagon and I fell off that wagon and broke my ass and dreams and I wake up the next morning in a field watching a cow watch me. With piss in my pants I make the long walk home past the HUD houses and abandoned cars and past the powwow grounds and the Assembly of God where the sinless sing like they could forgive us all. I get home and James is there with Suzy Song feeding him and rocking him like a boat or a three-legged chair.

I say no and I take James away and put him in his crib and I move into Suzy's arms and let her rock and rock me away from my stomach and thin skin.

1969

Long days and nights mean the sky looks the same all the time and James has no words yet but he dreams and kicks in his sleep and sometimes kicks his body against my body as he sleeps in my arms. Nobody dreams all the time because it would hurt too much but James keeps dreaming and sleeping through a summer rainstorm and heat lightning reaching down a hand and then a fist to tear a tree in half and then to tear my eyes in half with the light. We had venison for dinner. We ate deer and its wild taste shook me up and down my spine. James spit his mouthful out on the floor and the dogs came to finish it up and I ate and ate and the dogs ate and ate what they could find and the deer grew in my stomach. The deer grew horns and hooves and skin and eyes that pushed at my rib cage and I ate and ate

117

until I could not feel anything but my stomach expanding and stretched full.

All my life the days I remember most with every detail sharp and clear are the days when my stomach was full.

1969

We played our first basketball game of the season to-night in the community center and I had Suzy Song watch James while I played and all of us warriors roaring against the air and the nets and the clock that didn't work and our memories and our dreams and the twentieth-century horses we called our legs. We played some Nez Percé team and they ran like they were still running from the cavalry and they were kicking the shit out of us again when I suddenly steal the ball from their half-white point guard and drive all the way to the bucket. I jump in the air planning to dunk it when the half-white point guard runs under me knocking my ass to the floor and when I land I hear a crunch and my leg bends in half the wrong way. They take me to the reservation hospital and later on they tell me my leg has ex-ploded and I can't play ball for a long time or maybe forever and when Suzy comes by with James and they ask me if this is my wife and son and I tell them yes and James still doesn't make a noise and so they ask me how old he is. I tell them he's almost four years old and they say his physical development is slow but that's normal for an Indian child. Anyhow I have to have an operation and all but since I don't have the money or the strength or the memory and it's not covered by Indian Health I just get up and walk home almost crying because my leg and life hurt so bad. Suzy stays with me that night and in the dark she touches my knee and asks me how much it hurts and I tell her it hurts more than I can talk about so she kisses all my scars and she huddles up close to me and she's warm and she talks into my ear close. She isn't always asking questions and sometimes she has the answers. In the morning I wake up before her and I hobble into the kitchen and make some coffee and fix a couple of bowls of cornflakes and we sit in bed eating together while James lies still in his crib watching the ceiling so Suzy and I watch the ceiling too.

The ordinary can be like medicine.

1970

Early snow this year and James and I sit at home by the stove because I can't walk anywhere with my bad knee and since it is snowing so hard outside nobody could drive out to get us but I know somebody must be thinking about us because if they weren't we'd just disappear just like those Indians who used to climb the pueblos. Those Indians disappeared with food still cooking in the pot and air waiting to be breathed and they turned into birds or dust or the blue of the sky or the yellow of the sun.

There they were and suddenly they were forgotten for just a second and for just a second nobody thought about them and then they were gone.

1970

I took James down to the reservation hospital again because he was almost five years old and still hadn't bothered to talk yet or crawl or cry or even move when I put him on the floor and once I even dropped him and his head was bleeding and he didn't make a sound. They looked him over and said there was nothing wrong with him and that he's just a little slow developing and that's what the doctors always say and they've been saying that about Indians for five hundred years. Jesus I say don't you know that James wants to dance and to sing and to pound a drum so hard it hurts your ears and he ain't ever going to drop an eagle feather and he's always going to be respectful to elders at least the Indian elders and he's going to change the world. He's going to dynamite Mount Rushmore or hijack a plane and make it land on the reservation highway. He's going to be a father and a mother and a son and a daughter and a dog that will pull you from a raging river.

He'll make gold out of commodity cheese.

1970

Happy birthday James and I'm in the Breakaway Bar drinking too many beers when the Vietnam war comes on television. The white people always want to fight someone and they always get the dark-skinned people to do the fighting. All I know

120

about this war is what Seymour told me when he came back from his tour of duty over there and he said all the gooks he killed looked like us and Seymour said every single gook he killed looked exactly like someone he knew on the reservation. Anyhow I go to a Christmas party over at Jana Wind's house and leave James with my auntie so I could get really drunk and not have to worry about coming home for a few days or maybe for the rest of my life. We all get really drunk and Jana's old man Ray challenges me to a game of one-on-one since he says I'm for shit now and was never any good anyway but I tell him I can't since my knee is screwed up and besides there's two feet of snow on the ground and where are we going to play anyhow? Ray says I'm chickenshit so I tell him come on and we drive over to the high school to the outside court and there's two feet of snow on the court and we can't play but Ray smiles and pulls out a bottle of kerosene and pours it all over the court and lights it up and pretty soon the snow is all melted down along with most of Lester FallsApart's pants since he was standing too close to the court when Ray lit the fire. Anyhow the court is clear and Ray and I go at it and my knee only hurts a little and everyone was cheering us on and I can't remember who won since I was too drunk and so was everyone else. Later I hear how Ray and Joseph got arrested for beating some white guy half to death and I say that Ray and Joseph are just kids but Suzy says nobody on the reservation is ever a kid and that we're all born grown up anyway. I look at James and I think maybe Suzy is wrong about Indian kids being born adults and that maybe James was born this way and wants to stay this way like a baby because he doesn't want to grow up and see and do everything we all do?

There are all kinds of wars.

1971

So much time alone with a bottle of one kind or another and James and I remember nothing except the last drink and a drunk Indian is like the thinker statue except nobody puts a drunk Indian in a special place in front of a library. For most Indians the only special place in front of a library might be a heating grate or a piece of sun-warmed cement but that's an old joke and I used to sleep with my books in piles all over my bed and sometimes they were the only thing keeping me warm and always the only thing keeping me alive.

Books and beer are the best and worst defense.

1971

Jesse WildShoe died last night and today was the funeral and usually there's a wake but none of us had the patience or energy to mourn for days so we buried Jesse right away and dug the hole deep because Jesse could fancydance like God had touched his feet. Anyhow we dug the hole all day and since the ground was still a little frozen we kept doing the kerosene trick and melting the ice and frost and when we threw a match into the bottom of the grave it looked like I suppose hell must look and it was scary. There we were ten little Indians making a hell on earth for a fancydancer who already had enough of that shit and probably wouldn't want to have any more of it and I kept wondering if maybe we should just take his body high up in the mountains and bury him in the snow that never goes away. Maybe we just sort of freeze him so he doesn't have to feel anything anymore and especially not some crazy ideas of heaven or hell. I don't know anything about religion and I don't confess my sins to anybody except the walls and the wood stove and James who forgives everything like a rock. He ain't talking or crying at all and sometimes I shake him a little too hard or yell at him or leave him in his crib for hours all alone but he never makes a sound. One night I get so drunk I leave him at some-body's house and forget all about him and can you blame me? The tribal police drag me into the cell for abandonment and I'm asking them who they're going to arrest for abandoning me but the world is spinning and turning back on itself like a snake eating its own tail. Like a snake my TV dinner rises from the table the next day and snaps at my eyes and wrists and I ask the tribal cop how long I've been drunk and he tells me for most of a year and I don't remember any of it. I've got the DT's so bad and the walls are Nazis making lampshades out of my skin and the toilet is a white man in a white hood riding me down on horseback and the floor is a skinny man who wants to teach me a trick he's learned to do with a knife and my shoes squeal and kick and pull me down into the dead pig pit of my imagination. Oh Jesus I wake up on the bottom of that mass grave with the bones of generations of slaughter and I crawl and dig my way up through layers and years of the lunch special. I dig for hours through the skin and eyes and the fresh blood soon enough and pull myself through the eye of a sow and pluck the maggots from my hair and I want to scream but I don't want to open my mouth and taste and taste and taste.

Like the heroin addict said I just want to be pure.

1971

Been in A.A. for a month because that was the only way to keep James with me and my auntie and Suzy Song both moved into the house with me to make sure I don't drink and to help take care of James. They show the same old movies in A.A. and it's always the same white guy who almost destroys his life and his wife and his children and his job but finally realizes the alcohol is killing him and he quits overnight and spends the rest of the movie and the rest of his whole life at a picnic with his family and friends and boss all laughing and saying we didn't even recognize you back then Bob and we're glad to have you back Daddy and we'll hire you back at twice the salary you old dog you. Yesterday I get this postcard from Pine Ridge and my cousin says all the Indians there are gone and do I know where they went? I write back and tell him to look in the A.A. meeting and then I ask him if there are more birds with eyes that look like his and I ask him if the sky is more blue and the sun more yellow because those are the colors we all become when we die. I tell him to search his dreams for a man dressed in red with a red tie and red shoes and a hawk head. I tell him that man is fear and will eat you like a sandwich and will eat you like an ice cream cone and will never be full and he'll come for you in your dreams like he was a bad movie. I tell him to turn his television toward the wall and to study the walls for imperfections and those could be his mother and father and the stain on the ceiling could be his sisters and maybe the warped floorboard squeaking and squeaking is his grandfather talking stories.

Maybe they're all hiding on a ship in a bottle.

1972

Been sober so long it's like a dream but I feel better somehow and Auntie was so proud of me she took James and me into the city for James's checkup and James still wasn't talking but Auntie and James and I ate a great lunch at Woolworth's before we headed back to the reservation. I got to drive and Auntie's uranium money Cadillac is a hell of a car and it was raining a little and hot so there were rainbows rainbows rainbows and the pine trees looked like wise men with wet beards or at least I thought they did. That's how I do this life sometimes by making the ordinary just like magic and just like a card trick and just like a mirror and just like the disappearing. Every Indian learns how to be a magician and learns how to misdirect attention and the dark hand is always quicker than the white eye and no matter how close you get to my heart you will never find out my secrets and I'll never tell you and I'll never show you the same trick twice.

I'm traveling heavy with illusions.

1972

Every day I'm trying not to drink and I pray but I don't know who I'm praying to and if it's the basketball gathering ash on the shelf or the blank walls crushing me into the house or the television that only picks up public channels. I've seen only painters and fishermen and I think they're both the same kind of men who made a different choice one time in their lives. The fisherman held a rod in his hand and said yes and the painter held a brush in his hand and said yes and sometimes I hold a beer in my hand and say yes. At those moments I want to drink so bad that it aches and I cry which is a strange noise in our house because James refuses tears and he refuses words but sometimes he holds a hand up above his head like he's reaching for something. Yesterday I nearly trip over Lester FallsApart lying drunk as a skunk in front of the Trading Post and I pick him up and he staggers and trembles and falls back down. Lester I say you got to stand up on your own and I pick him up and he falls down again.

Only a saint would have tried to pick him up the third time.

1972

The streetlight outside my house shines on tonight and I'm watching it like it could give me vision. James ain't talked ever and he looks at that streetlight like it was a word and maybe like it was a verb. James wanted to streetlight me and make me bright and beautiful so all the moths and bats would circle me like I was the center of the world and held secrets. Like Joy said that everything but humans keeps secrets. Today I get my mail and there's a light bill and a postcard from an old love from Seattle who asks me if I still love her like I used to and would I come to visit?

I send her my light bill and tell her I don't ever want to see her again.

1973

James talked today but I had my back turned and I couldn't be sure it was real. He said potato like any good Indian would because that's all we eat. But maybe he said I love you because that's what I wanted him to say or maybe he said geology or mathematics or college basketball. I pick him up and ask him again and again what did you say? He just smiles and I take him to the clinic and the doctors say it's about time but are you sure you didn't imagine his voice? I said James's voice sounded like a beautiful glass falling off the shelf and landing safely on a thick shag carpet.

The doctor said I had a very good imagination.

1973

I'm shooting hoops again with the younger Indian boys and even some Indian girls who never miss a shot. They call me old man and elder and give me a little bit of respect like not running too fast or hard and even letting me shoot a few more than I should. It's been a long time since I played but the old feelings and old moves are there in my heart and in my fingers. I see these Indian kids and I know that basketball was invented by an Indian long before that Naismith guy ever thought about it. When I play I don't feel like drinking so I wish I could play twenty-four hours a day seven days a week and then I wouldn't wake up shaking and quaking and needing just one more beer before I stop for good. James knows it too and he sits on the sideline clapping when my team scores and clapping when the other team scores too. He's got a good heart. He always talks whenever I'm not in the room or I'm not looking at him but never when anybody else might hear so they all think I'm crazy. I am crazy. He says things like I can't believe. He says $E = MC^2$ and that's why all my cousins drink themselves to death. He says the earth is an oval marble that nobody can win. He says the sky is not blue and the grass is not green.

He says everything is a matter of perception.

1973

Christmas and James gets his presents and he gives me the best present of all when he talks right at me. He says so many things and the only thing that matters is that he says he and I don't have the right to die for each other and that we should be living for each other instead. He says the world hurts. He says the first thing he wanted after he was born was a shot of whiskey. He says all that and more. He tells me to get a job and to grow my braids. He says I better learn how to shoot left-handed if I'm going to keep playing basketball. He says to open a fireworks stand.

Every day now there are little explosions all over the reservation.

1974

Today is the World's Fair in Spokane and James and I drive to Spokane with a few cousins of mine. All the countries have exhibitions like art from Japan and pottery from Mexico and mean-looking people talking about Germany. In one little corner there's a statue of an Indian who's supposed to be some chief or another. I press a little button and the statue talks and moves its arms over and over in the same motion. The statue tells the crowd we have to take care of the earth because it is our mother. I know that and James says he knows more. He says the earth is our grandmother and that technology has become our mother and that they both hate each other. James tells the crowd that the river just a few yards from where we stand is all we ever need to believe in. One white woman asks me how old James is and I tell her he's seven and she tells me that he's so smart for an Indian boy. James hears this and tells the white woman that she's pretty smart for an old white woman. I know this is how it will all begin and how the rest of my life will be. I know when I am old and sick and ready to die that James will wash my body and take care of my wastes. He'll carry me from HUD house to sweathouse and he will clean my wounds. And he will talk and teach me something new every day.

But all that is so far ahead.

A TRAIN IS AN ORDER OF OCCURRENCE DESIGNED TO LEAD TO SOME RESULT

there is something about
trains, drinking, and being
an indian with nothing to lose.
—Ray Young Bear

"Broom, dustpan, sweep, trash can," Samuel Builds-the-Fire chanted as he showered and shaved, combed his hair into braids. Samuel was a maid at a motel on Third Avenue. He wanted to be early to work this morning because it was his birthday. But he didn't expect any presents or party from his co-workers, from the management. Being really early to work that morning was a kind of gift to himself.

The walk from his studio apartment on Hospital Row to downtown only took five minutes on a sunny day and four minutes on a rainy day, but Samuel left home nearly half an hour before he was supposed to clock in. "Early, early, real early," he chanted. It was a good day: sun, light wind, and small noises like laughter from open car windows and fast-food restaurants.

All the previous week, Samuel had opened his mailbox expecting to find a card or letter from his children. *Happy Birthday* from Gallup; *Best Wishes* from Anchorage; *I Love You* from Fort Bliss, Texas. Nothing had arrived, though, and Samuel was hurt some. But he understood that his children were busy, busy, busy.

"Got their own fry bread cooking in the oven. Got a whole lot of feathers in their warbonnets," Samuel said as he walked into the motel.

"Oh, Samuel," the motel manager said. "You're early. Good. We need to talk."

Samuel followed the manager into the back office. They both sat down at the big desk, Samuel on one side and the manager on the other.

"Samuel," the manager said. "I don't know exactly how to tell you this. But I'm going to have to let you go."

"Excuse me, sir?" Samuel said. He was sure the manager had said something entirely different.

"Samuel, this damn recession is hurting everyone. I need to cut back on expenses, trim the sails. You understand, don't you?"

Samuel understood. He picked up his severance check and headed for the door.

"Samuel," the manager said. "As soon as things get better, you'll be the first one I call. I guarantee that. You've been an outstanding employee."

"Thank you, sir," Samuel said as he walked out the door. Halfway down the block toward home, he stopped. He realized he had forgotten to tell the manager it was his birthday. For a moment, Samuel was convinced that would change everything. But no, Samuel knew it was over. The Third Avenue Motel's rooms numbers one through twenty-seven would never be clean, not clean like Samuel knew how to make them. Hell, he re-created those rooms for each new guest.

Samuel Builds-the-Fire was father to Samuel Builds-the-Fire, Jr., who was father to Thomas Builds-the-Fire. They all had the gift of storytelling, could pick up the pieces of a story from the street and change the world for a few moments. When Samuel was younger, before he was even a husband and father, he would win bets by telling stories constructed by random objects. Once, he walked with friends in Riverfront Park in Spokane and they all saw a duck swoop down and pick up an abandoned hot dog. At the same time, a white mother pulled her son from the edge of the river.

"Tell us a story about all that," his friends said. "And if it's good, we'll give you ten bucks."

"Twenty," Samuel said.

"Deal."

"Real deal," Samuel said and closed his eyes for a moment. "This young Indian boy, tired and hungry, steals a hot dog from a sidewalk vendor. He runs away and the vendor chases him through the park. The Indian boy drops the hot dog and jumps into the river. He cannot swim, though, and drowns quickly. The vendor sees what he has caused by his greed, changes himself into a duck, grabs the hot dog, and flies away. Meanwhile, a little white boy watches all this happen and leans over the water to see the Indian boy's body wait at the bottom of the river. His mother refuses to believe him, though, and takes him away, kicking and screaming, into the end of the story."

Samuel opened his eyes and his friends cheered, gave him the twenty bucks and some extra change.

"Some good old pocket money," Samuel said and bought each of his friends a hot dog.

"What was God but this planet's maid?" Samuel asked himself as he found himself walking to the Midway Tavern, where all the Indians drank in eight-hour shifts. Samuel hadn't ever been fired from a job and he had never been in a bar, either. He had never drunk. All his life he had watched his brothers and sisters, most of his tribe, fall into alcoholism and surrendered dreams.

But today Samuel sat down at the bar, unsure of himself, frightened.

"Hey, partner," the bartender said to Samuel. "Ain't seen you in here before."

"Yeah," Samuel said. "Just got into town, you know?"

"Where you from?"

"A long way from here. Doubt you ever heard of it."

"Oh, I know all about that place," the bartender said and set a cocktail napkin in front of Samuel. "So, what you are drinking, old-timer?"

"I'm not sure. Do you have a menu?"

The bartender laughed and laughed. Embarrassed, Samuel wanted to get up and run home. But he sat still, waited for the laughter to end.

"How about I just give you a beer?" the bartender asked then, and Samuel quickly agreed.

The bartender set the beer in front of Samuel; the bartender laughed and had the urge to call the local newspaper. *You got to get a photographer here. This Injun is going to take his first drink.*

Samuel lifted the glass. It felt good and cold in his hand. He drank. Coughed. Set the glass down for a second. Lifted it again. Drank. Drank. Held the glass away from his mouth. Breathed. Breathed. He drank. Emptied the glass. Set it down gently on the bar.

I understand everything, Samuel thought. He knew all about how it begins; he knew he wanted to live this way now.

With each glass of beer, Samuel gained a few ounces of wisdom, courage. But after a while, he began to understand too much about fear and failure, too. At the halfway point of any drunken night, there is a moment when an Indian realizes he cannot turn back toward tradition and that he has no map to guide him toward the future.

"Shit," Samuel said. It was quickly his favorite word.

Samuel had always thought alcohol would corrupt his stories, render them useless, flat. He knew his stories had the power to teach, to show how this life should be lived. He would often tell his children and their friends, and then his grandchildren and their friends, those stories which could make their worlds into something better. At the very least, he could tell funny stories that would make each day less painful.

"Listen," Samuel said. "Coyote, who is the creator of all

134

of us, was sitting on his cloud the day after he created the Indians. Now, he liked the Indians, liked what they were doing. *This is good,* he kept saying to himself. But he was bored. He thought and thought about what he should make next in the world. But he couldn't think of anything so he decided to clip his toenails. He clipped his right toenails and held the clippings in his right hand. Then he clipped his left toenails and added those clippings to the ones already in his right hand. He looked around and around his cloud for somewhere to throw away his clippings. But he couldn't find anywhere and he got mad. He started jumping up and down because he was so mad. Then he accidentally dropped his toenail clippings over the side of the cloud and they fell to the earth. The clippings burrowed into the ground like seeds and grew up to be the white man. Coyote, he looked down at his newest creation and said, *Oh, shit.*"

"The whites are crazy, the whites are crazy," the children would chant and dance around Samuel in circles.

"And sometimes so are the Indians," Samuel would whisper to himself.

After Samuel had taught his children everything he could, everything he knew, they left him alone. Just like white kids. Samuel lived on the reservation, alone, for as long as he could, without money or company. All his friends had died and all the younger people on the reservation had no time for stories. Samuel felt like the horse must have felt when Henry Ford came along.

When Samuel finally did move into Spokane, he could only find a small studio apartment. But it was more than enough.

135

The first thing he did was to fill the four corners of the room with plaster, to make them round. He painted a black circle in the middle of the ceiling that looked like the smoke hole of a tipi. His little studio looked like the inside of a tipi. It felt like home. Something close to home, at least.

He went down to the Third Avenue Motel first thing and applied for a job as a desk clerk. But the manager said he needed a maid.

"I hear you Indian men do good housework," the manager said.

"Well," Samuel said. "I don't know about other Indians but I know how to keep a clean house."

"Good," the manager said. "I can't pay you much, though. Just minimum wage."

"Good enough."

When Samuel first started work, the Third Avenue Motel was semirespectable. By the time he was fired, it was a home for drug dealers and prostitutes.

"Why do you let those people in here?" Samuel asked the manager more than once.

"They pay their bills," the manager always said.

Sometimes an Indian woman would work out of the motel and that always hurt Samuel more than anything he could ever imagine. In his dreams, he would see his own daughter's face in the faces of the prostitutes.

On paydays, Samuel would give the Indian prostitutes a little money.

"Don't work today," he would say. "Just for today."

Sometimes the Indian women would take his money and

work anyway. But, once in a while, one of those Indian prostitutes would take the money and go drink coffee in Denny's all day instead of working. Those were good days for Samuel.

A year before he was fired, Samuel found a young Indian boy dead in room sixteen. Drug overdose. Samuel sat in the room and studied the boy's face until the police arrived. Samuel wanted to know what tribe the boy was and couldn't be sure. His eyes were Yakima but his nose was Lakota. Maybe he was mixed-blood.

When the police came and lifted the Indian boy from the bed with a tearing and stretching sound that nearly broke Samuel's eardrums, the stories waiting to be told left and never returned. All Samuel could do after that was hum and sing songs he already knew or songs that made no sense.

At closing time, Samuel was pushed out the door into the street. He staggered from locked door to locked door, believing that any open door meant he was home. He pissed his pants. He couldn't believe he lost his job. He climbed up an embankment and stood on the Union Pacific Railroad tracks that passed through and over the middle of the city.

Samuel was elevated exactly fourteen feet and seven inches above the rest of the world.

He heard the whistle in the distance; it sounded like horses stampeding. "Im your horse in the night," Samuel sang that Gal Costa song. He sang, "I'm your horse in the night."

The whistle grew louder, angry.

Samuel tripped on a rail, fell face down on the tracks.

The whistle. The whistle. The tracks vibrated, rattled like bones in a stick game. *Is it hidden in the left hand or the right hand?* Samuel closed his hands and his eyes.

Sometimes it's called passing out and sometimes it's just pretending to be asleep.

A GOOD STORY

THE QUILTING

A quiet Saturday reservation afternoon and I pretend sleep on the couch while my mother pieces together another quilt on the living room floor.

"You know," she says. "Those stories you tell, they're kind of sad, enit?"

I keep my eyes closed.

"Junior," she says. "Don't you think your stories are too sad?"

My efforts to ignore her are useless.

"What do you mean?" I ask.

She puts down her scissors and fabric, looks at me so straight that I have to sit up and open my eyes.

"Well," she says. "Ain't nobody cries that much, you know?"

I pretend to rub the sleep from my eyes, stretch my arms and legs, make small noises of irritation.

"I guess," I say. "But ain't nobody laughs as much as the people in my stories, either."

"That's true," she says.

I stand up, shake my pants loose, and walk to the kitchen to grab a Diet Pepsi with cold, cold ice.

Mom quilts silently for a while. Then she whistles.

"What?" I ask her, knowing these signals for attention.

"You know what you should do? You should write a story about something good, a real good story."

"Why?"

"Because people should know that good things always happen to Indians, too."

I take a big drink of Diet Pepsi, search the cupboards for potato chips, peanuts, anything.

"Good things happen," she says and goes back to her quilting.

I think for a moment, put my Diet Pepsi down on the counter.

"Okay," I say. "If you want to hear a good story, you have to listen."

140

THE STORY

Uncle Moses sat in his sandwich chair eating a sandwich. Between bites, he hummed an it-is-a-good-day song. He sat in front of the house he built himself fifty years before. The house sat down at random angles to the ground. The front room leaned to the west, the bedroom to the east, and the bathroom simply folded in on itself.

There was no foundation, no hidden closet, nothing built into the thin walls. On the whole, it was the kind of house that would stand even years after Moses died, held up by the tribal imagination. Driving by, the Indians would look across the field toward the house and hold it upright with their eyes, remembering *Moses lived there.*

It would be just enough to ensure survival.

Uncle Moses gave no thought to his passing on most days. Instead, he usually finished his sandwich, held the last bite of bread and meat in his mouth like the last word of a good story.

"Ya-hey," he called out to the movement of air, the unseen. A summer before, Uncle Moses listened to his nephew, John-John, talking a story. John-John was back from college and told Moses that 99 percent of the matter in the universe is invisible to the human eye. Ever since, Moses made sure to greet what he could not see.

Uncle Moses stood, put his hands on his hips, arched his back. More and more, he heard his spine playing stickgame through his skin, singing old dusty words, the words of all his years. He looked at the position of the sun to determine the time, checked his watch to be sure, and looked across the field for the children who would soon come.

The Indian children would come with half-braids, curiosity endless and essential. The children would come from throwing stones into water, from basketball and basketry, from the arms of their mothers and fathers, from the very beginning. This was the generation of HUD house, of car wreck and cancer, of commodity cheese and beef. These were the children who carried dreams in the back pockets of their blue jeans, pulled them out easily, traded back and forth.

"Dreams like baseball cards," Uncle Moses said to himself, smiled hard when he saw the first child running across the field. It was Arnold, of course, pale-skinned boy who was always teased by the other children.

Arnold ran slowly, his great belly shaking with the effort, eyes narrowed in concentration. A full-blood Spokane, Arnold was somehow born with pale, pretty skin and eyes with color continually changing from gray to brown. He liked to sit in the sandwich chair and wait for Uncle Moses to make him a good sandwich.

It took Arnold five minutes to run across the field, and all the while Moses watched him, studied his movements, the way Arnold's hair reached out in all directions, uncombed, so close to electricity, closer to lightning. He did not wear braids, could not sit long enough for his mother.

Be still, be still, she would say between her teeth, but Arnold loved his body too much to remain still.

Big as he was, Arnold was still graceful in his movements, in his hands when he touched his face listening to a good story. He was also the best basketball player in the reservation grade school. Uncle Moses sometimes walked to the playground just to watch Arnold play and wonder at the strange, often improbable gifts a person can receive.

We are all given something to compensate for what we have lost. Moses felt those words even though he did not say them.

Arnold arrived, breathing hard.

"Ya-hey, Little Man," Uncle Moses said.

"Hello, Uncle," Arnold replied, extending his hand in a half-shy, half-adult way, a child's greeting, the affirmation of friendship.

"Where are the others?" Uncle Moses asked, taking Arnold's hand in his own.

"There was a field trip," Arnold answered. "All the others went to a baseball game in Spokane. I hid until they left."

"Why?"

"Because I wanted to see you."

Moses smiled at Arnold's unplanned kindness. He held the child's hand a little tighter and pulled him up close.

"Little Man," he said. "You have done a good thing."

Arnold smiled, pulled his hand away from Moses, and covered his smile, smiling even harder.

"Uncle Moses," he said through his fingers. "Tell me a good story."

Uncle Moses sat down in the story chair and told this very story.

THE FINISHING

My mother sits quietly, rips a seam, begins to hum a slow song through her skinny lips.

"What you singing?" I ask.

"I'm singing an it-is-a-good-day song."

She smiles and I have to smile with her.

"Did you like the story?" I ask.

She keeps singing, sings a little louder and stronger as I take my Diet Pepsi outside and wait in the sun. It is warm, soon to be cold, but that's in the future, maybe tomorrow, probably the next day and all the days after that. Today, now, I drink what I have, will eat what is left in the cupboard, while my mother finishes her quilt, piece by piece.

Believe me, there is just barely enough goodness in all of this.

THE FIRST ANNUAL ALL-INDIAN HORSESHOE PITCH AND BARBECUE

S omebody forgot the charcoal; blame the BIA.

I've never heard any Indian play the piano until Victor bought a secondhand baby grand at a flea market and hauled it out to the reservation in the back of a BIA pickup. All that summer the piano collected spiders and warm rain, until it swelled like a good tumor. I asked him over and over, "Victor, when you going to play that thing?" He would smile, mumble some unintelligible prayer, and then whisper to me close, "There

is a good day to die and there is a good day to play the piano."
Just before the barbecue Victor pushed the piano halfway across
the reservation, up against a pine tree, flexed his muscles,
cracked his knuckles, sat down at the keys, and pounded out
Béla Bartók. In the long silence after Victor finished his piece,
after the beautiful dissonance and implied survival, the Spokane
Indians wept, stunned by this strange and familiar music.

"Well," Lester FallsApart said. "It ain't Hank Williams
but I know what it means."

Then Nadine said, "You can tell so much about a family
by whether their piano is in or out of tune."

There is something beautiful about the cool grass beneath a picnic table. I was there, almost asleep, when my love
crawled under, wrapped her arms around me, and sang into my
ear. Her breath sweet and damp with Kool-Aid and a hot dog,
mustard but no catsup, please. The sunlight squeezed through
spaces between wood, fell down knotholes, but just enough to
warm my face.

There is something beautiful about an Indian boy with
hair so black it collects the sunlight. His braids grow hot to the
touch and his skin shines with reservation sweat. He is skinny
and doesn't know how to spit. In the foot race with other Indian boys he wins a blue ribbon, and in the wrestling match he
wins a medallion with an eagle etched in cheap metal. There
are photographs taken; I use them now as evidence of his
smile.

There is something beautiful about broken glass and the
tiny visions it creates. For instance, the glass from that shattered

beer bottle told me there was a twenty-dollar bill hidden in the center of an ant pile. I buried my arms elbow-deep in the ants but all I found was a note that said *Some people will believe in anything.* And I laughed.

There is something beautiful about an ordinary carnival.

Simon won the horseshoe pitch with a double-ringer that was so perfect we all knew his grandchildren would still be telling the story, and Simon won the storytelling contest when he told us the salmon used to swim so thick in the Spokane River that an Indian could walk across the water on their backs.

"You don't think Jesus Christ was walking on just faith?" he asked us all.

Simon won the coyote contest when he told us that basketball should be our new religion.

He said, "A ball bouncing on hardwood sounds like a drum."

He said, "An all-star jacket makes you one of the Shirt Wearers."

Simon won the one-on-one basketball tournament with a jump shot from one hundred years out.

"Do you think it's any coincidence that basketball was invented just one year after the Ghost Dancers fell at Wounded Knee?" he asked me and you.

And then Seymour told Simon, "Winning all those contests makes you just about as famous as the world's best xylophone player."

All the Indians were running; they were running. There was no fear, no pain. It was the pleasure of bare foot inside tennis shoe; it was the pleasure of tennis shoe on red dirt.

That Skin with the long hair leaning against the pine tree, *yes, that one*, is in love with that other Skin sitting at the picnic table drinking a Pepsi. Neither has the words to describe this but they know how to dance, *yes, they know how to dance*.

Can you hear the dreams crackling like a campfire? Can you hear the dreams sweeping through the pine trees and tipis? Can you hear the dreams laughing in the sawdust? Can you hear the dreams shaking just a little bit as the day grows long? Can you hear the dreams putting on a good jacket that smells of fry bread and sweet smoke? Can you hear the dreams stay up late and talk so many stories?

And finally this, when the sun was falling down so beautiful we didn't have time to give it a name, she held the child born of white mother and red father and said, "Both sides of this baby are beautiful."

IMAGINING THE
RESERVATION

We have to believe in the power of imagination
because it's all we have, and ours is stronger
than theirs.
—Lawrence Thornton

I magine Crazy Horse invented the atom bomb in 1876 and detonated it over Washington, D.C. Would the urban Indians still be sprawled around the one-room apartment in the cable television reservation? Imagine a loaf of bread could feed the entire tribe. Didn't you know Jesus Christ was a Spokane Indian? Imagine Columbus landed in 1492 and some tribe or another drowned him in the ocean. Would Lester FallsApart still be shoplifting in the 7-11?

*   *   *

I am in the 7-11 of my dreams, surrounded by five hundred years of convenient lies. There are men here who take inventory, scan the aisles for minute changes, insist on small bills. Once, I worked the graveyard shift in a Seattle 7-11, until the night a man locked me in the cooler and stole all the money out of the cash register. But more than that, he took the dollar bill from my wallet, pulled the basketball shoes off my feet, and left me waiting for rescue between the expired milk and broken eggs. It was then I remembered the story of the hobo who hopped a train heading west, found himself locked in a refrigerator car, and froze to death. He was discovered when the train arrived at its final destination, his body ice cold, but the refrigerator car was never turned on, the temperature inside never dropped below fifty degrees. It happens that way: the body forgets the rhythm of survival.

Survival = Anger × Imagination. Imagination is the only weapon on the reservation.

The reservation doesn't sing anymore but the songs still hang in the air. Every molecule waits for a drumbeat; every element dreams lyrics. Today I am walking between water, two parts hydrogen, one part oxygen, and the energy expelled is named *Forgiveness*.

The Indian child hears my voice on the telephone and he knows what color shirt I'm wearing. A few days or years ago, my brother and I took him to the bar and he read all of our futures by touching hands. He told me the twenty-dollar bill hidden in my shoe would change my life. *Imagine,* he said. But we all laughed, old Moses even spit his false teeth into the air, but the Indian child touched another hand, another, and another, until he touched every Skin. *Who do you think you are?* Seymour asked the Indian child. *You ain't some medicine man come back to change our lives.* But the Indian child told Seymour his missing daughter was in community college in San Francisco and his missing wedding ring was in a can of commodity beef high up in his kitchen. The Indian child told Lester his heart was buried at the base of a pine tree behind the Trading Post. The Indian child told me to break every mirror in my house and tape the pieces to my body. I followed his vision and the Indian child laughed and laughed when he saw me, reflecting every last word of the story.

What do you believe in? Does every Indian depend on Hollywood for a twentieth-century vision? Listen: when I was young, living on the reservation, eating potatoes every day of my life, I imagined the potatoes grew larger, filled my stomach, reversed the emptiness. My sisters saved up a few quarters and bought food coloring. For weeks we ate red potatoes, green potatoes, blue potatoes. In the dark, "The Tonight Show" on the television, my father and I telling stories about the food we wanted most. We imagined oranges, Pepsi-Cola, chocolate, deer jerky. We imagined the salt on our skin could change the world.

* * *

July 4th and all is hell. Adrian, I am waiting for someone to tell the truth. Today I am celebrating the Indian boy who blew his fingers off when an M80 exploded in his hand. But thank God for miracles, he has a thumb left to oppose his future. I am celebrating Tony Swaggard, sleeping in the basement with two thousand dollars' worth of fireworks when some spark of flame or history touched it all off. Driving home, I heard the explosion and thought it was a new story born. But, Adrian, it's the same old story, whispered past the same false teeth. How can we imagine a new language when the language of the enemy keeps our dismembered tongues tied to his belt? How can we imagine a new alphabet when the old jumps off billboards down into our stomachs? Adrian, what did you say? *I want to rasp into sober cryptology and say something dynamic but tonight is my laundry night.* How do we imagine a new life when a pocketful of quarters weighs our possibilities down?

There are so many possibilities in the reservation 7-11, so many methods of survival. Imagine every Skin on the reservation is the new lead guitarist for the Rolling Stones, on the cover of a rock-and-roll magazine. Imagine forgiveness is sold 2 for 1. Imagine every Indian is a video game with braids. Do you believe laughter can save us? All I know is that I count coyotes to help me sleep. Didn't you know? Imagination is the politics of dreams; imagination turns every word into a bottle rocket. Adrian, imagine every day is Independence Day and save us from traveling the river changed; save us from hitchhiking the long road home. Imagine an escape. Imagine that your own shadow on the wall is a perfect door. Imagine a song stronger than penicillin. Imagine a spring with water that mends broken bones. Imagine a drum which wraps itself around your heart. Imagine a story that puts wood in the fireplace.

THE APPROXIMATE SIZE
OF MY FAVORITE TUMOR

A fter the argument that I had lost but pretended to win, I stormed out of the HUD house, jumped into the car, and prepared to drive off in victory, which was also known as defeat. But I realized that I hadn't grabbed my keys. At that kind of moment, a person begins to realize how he can be fooled by his own games. And at that kind of moment, a person begins to formulate a new game to compensate for the failure of the first.

"Honey, I'm home," I yelled as I walked back into the house.

My wife ignored me, gave me a momentary stoic look

that impressed me with its resemblance to generations of television Indians.

"Oh, what is that?" I asked. "Your Tonto face?"

She flipped me off, shook her head, and disappeared into the bedroom.

"Honey," I called after her. "Didn't you miss me? I've been gone so long and it's good to be back home. Where I belong."

I could hear dresser drawers open and close.

"And look at the kids," I said as I patted the heads of imagined children. "They've grown so much. And they have your eyes."

She walked out of the bedroom in her favorite ribbon shirt, hair wrapped in her best ties, and wearing a pair of come-here boots. You know, the kind with the curled toe that looks like a finger gesturing *Come here, cowboy, come on over here.* But those boots weren't meant for me: I'm an Indian.

"Honey," I asked. "I just get back from the war and you're leaving already? No kiss for the returning hero?"

She pretended to ignore me, which I enjoyed. But then she pulled out her car keys, checked herself in the mirror, and headed for the door. I jumped in front of her, knowing she meant to begin her own war. That scared the shit out of me.

"Hey," I said. "I was just kidding, honey. I'm sorry. I didn't mean anything. I'll do whatever you want me to."

She pushed me aside, adjusted her dreams, pulled on her braids for a jumpstart, and walked out the door. I followed her and stood on the porch as she jumped into the car and started it up.

"I'm going dancing," she said and drove off into the

sunset, or at least she drove down the tribal highway toward the Powwow Tavern.

"But what am I going to feed the kids?" I asked and walked back into the house to feed myself and my illusions.

After a dinner of macaroni and commodity cheese, I put on my best shirt, a new pair of blue jeans, and set out to hitchhike down the tribal highway. The sun had gone down already so I decided that I was riding off toward the great unknown, which was actually the same Powwow Tavern where my love had escaped to an hour earlier.

As I stood on the highway with my big, brown, and beautiful thumb showing me the way, Simon pulled up in his pickup, stopped, opened the passenger door, and whooped.

"Shit," he yelled. "If it ain't little Jimmy One-Horse! Where you going, cousin, and how fast do you need to get there?"

I hesitated at the offer of a ride. Simon was world famous, at least famous on the Spokane Indian Reservation, for driving backward. He always obeyed posted speed limits, traffic signals and signs, even minute suggestions. But he drove in reverse, using the rearview mirror as his guide. But what could I do? I trusted the man, and when you trust a man you also have to trust his horse.

"I'm headed for the Powwow Tavern," I said and climbed into Simon's rig. "And I need to be there before my wife finds herself a dance partner."

"Shit," Simon said. "Why didn't you say something sooner? We'll be there before she hears the first note of the first goddamned song."

Simon jammed the car into his only gear, reverse, and

156

roared down the highway. I wanted to hang my head out the window like a dog, let my braids flap like a tongue in the wind, but good manners prevented me from taking the liberty. Still, it was so tempting. Always was.

"So, little Jimmy Sixteen-and-One-Half-Horses," Simon asked me after a bit. "What did you do to make your wife take off this time?"

"Well," I said. "I told her the truth, Simon. I told her I got cancer everywhere inside me."

Simon slammed on the brakes and brought the pickup sliding to a quick but decidedly cinematic stop.

"That ain't nothing to joke about," he yelled.

"Ain't joking about the cancer," I said. "But I started joking about dying and that pissed her off."

"What'd you say?"

"Well, I told her the doctor showed me my X-rays and my favorite tumor was just about the size of a baseball, shaped like one, too. Even had stitch marks."

"You're full of shit."

"No, really. I told her to call me Babe Ruth. Or Roger Maris. Maybe even Hank Aaron 'cause there must have been about 755 damn tumors inside me. Then, I told her I was going to Cooperstown and sit right down in the lobby of the Hall of Fame. Make myself a new exhibit, you know? Pin my X-rays to my chest and point out the tumors. What a dedicated baseball fan! What a sacrifice for the national pastime!"

"You're an asshole, little Jimmy Zero-Horses."

"I know, I know," I said as Simon got the pickup rolling again, down the highway toward an uncertain future, which was, as usual, simply called the Powwow Tavern.

We rode the rest of the way in silence. That is to say that neither of us had anything at all to say. But I could hear Simon breathing and I'm sure he could hear me, too. And once, he coughed.

"There you go, cousin," he said finally as he stopped his pickup in front of the Powwow Tavern. "I hope it all works out, you know?"

I shook his hand, offered him a few exaggerated gifts, made a couple promises that he knew were just promises, and waved wildly as he drove off, backwards, and away from the rest of my life. Then I walked into the tavern, shook my body like a dog shaking off water. I've always wanted to walk into a bar that way.

"Where the hell is Suzy Boyd?" I asked.

"Right here, asshole," Suzy answered quickly and succinctly.

"Okay, Suzy," I asked. "Where the hell is my wife?"

"Right here, asshole," my wife answered quickly and succinctly. Then she paused a second before she added, "And quit calling me *your wife*. It makes me sound like I'm a fucking bowling ball or something."

"Okay, okay, Norma," I said and sat down beside her. I ordered a Diet Pepsi for me and a pitcher of beer for the next table. There was no one sitting at the next table. It was just something I always did. Someone would come along and drink it.

"Norma," I said. "I'm sorry. I'm sorry I have cancer and I'm sorry I'm dying."

She took a long drink of her Diet Pepsi, stared at me for a long time. Stared hard.

158

"Are you going to make any more jokes about it?" she asked.

"Just one or two more, maybe," I said and smiled. It was exactly the wrong thing to say. Norma slapped me in anger, had a look of concern for a moment as she wondered what a slap could do to a person with terminal cancer, and then looked angry again.

"If you say anything funny ever again, I'm going to leave you," Norma said. "And I'm fucking serious about that."

I lost my smile briefly, reached across the table to hold her hand, and said something incredibly funny. It was maybe the best one-liner I had ever uttered. Maybe the moment that would have made me a star anywhere else. But in the Powwow Tavern, which was just a front for reality, Norma heard what I had to say, stood up, and left me.

Because Norma left me, it's even more important to know how she arrived in my life.

I was sitting in the Powwow Tavern on a Saturday night with my Diet Pepsi and my second-favorite cousin, Raymond.

"Look it, look it," he said as Norma walked into the tavern. Norma was over six feet tall. Well, maybe not six feet tall but she was taller than me, taller than everyone in the bar except the basketball players.

"What tribe you think she is?" Raymond asked me.

"Amazon," I said.

"Their reservation down by Santa Fe, enit?" Raymond asked, and I laughed so hard that Norma came over to find out about the commotion.

"Hello, little brothers," she said. "Somebody want to buy me a drink?"

"What you having?" I asked.

"Diet Pepsi," she said and I knew we would fall in love.

"Listen," I told her. "If I stole 1,000 horses, I'd give you 501 of them."

"And what other women would get the other 499?" she asked.

And we laughed. Then we laughed harder when Raymond leaned in closer to the table and said, "I don't get it."

Later, after the tavern closed, Norma and I sat outside on my car and shared a cigarette. I should say that we pretended to share a cigarette since neither of us smoked. But we both thought the other did and wanted to have all that much more in common.

After an hour or two of coughing, talking stories, and laughter, we ended up at my HUD house, watching late-night television. Raymond was passed out in the backseat of my car.

"Hey," she said. "That cousin of yours ain't too smart."

"Yeah," I said. "But he's cool, you know?"

"Must be. Because you're so good to him."

"He's my cousin, you know? That's how it is."

She kissed me then. Soft at first. Then harder. Our teeth clicked together like it was a junior high kiss. Still, we sat on the couch and kissed until the television signed off and broke into white noise. It was the end of another broadcast day.

"Listen," I said then. "I should take you home."

"Home?" she asked. "I thought I was at home."

"Well, my tipi is your tipi," I said, and she lived there until the day I told her that I had terminal cancer.

160

I have to mention the wedding, though. It was at the Spokane Tribal Longhouse and all my cousins and her cousins were there. Nearly two hundred people. Everything went smoothly until my second-favorite cousin, Raymond, drunk as a skunk, stood up in the middle of the ceremony, obviously confused.

"I remember Jimmy real good," Raymond said and started into his eulogy for me as I stood not two feet from him. "Jimmy was always quick with a joke. Make you laugh all the damn time. I remember once at my grandmother's wake, he was standing by the coffin. Now, you got to remember he was only seven or eight years old. Anyway, he starts jumping up and down, yelling, *She moved, she moved.*"

Everyone at the wedding laughed because it was pretty much the same crowd that was at the funeral. Raymond smiled at his newly discovered public speaking ability and continued.

"Jimmy was always the one to make people feel better, too," he said. "I remember once when he and I were drinking at the Powwow Tavern when all of a sudden Lester FallsApart comes running in and says that ten Indians just got killed in a car wreck on Ford Canyon Road. *Ten Skins?* I asked Lester, and he said, *Yeah, ten.* And then Jimmy starts up singing, *One little, two little, three little Indians, four little, five little, six little Indians, seven little, eight little, nine little Indians, ten little Indian boys.*"

Everyone in the wedding laughed some more, but also looked a little tense after that story, so I grabbed Raymond and led him back to his seat. He stared incredulously at me, tried to reconcile his recent eulogy with my sudden appearance. He just sat there until the preacher asked that most rhetorical of questions:

"And if there is anyone here who has objections to this union, speak now or forever hold your peace."

Raymond staggered and stumbled to his feet, then staggered and stumbled up to the preacher.

"Reverend," Raymond said. "I hate to interrupt, but my cousin is dead, you know? I think that might be a problem."

Raymond passed out at that moment, and Norma and I were married with his body draped unceremoniously over our feet.

Three months after Norma left me, I lay in my hospital bed in Spokane, just back from another stupid and useless radiation treatment.

"Jesus," I said to my attending physician. "A few more zaps and I'll be Superman."

"Really?" the doctor said. "I never realized that Clark Kent was a Spokane Indian."

And we laughed, you know, because sometimes that's all two people have in common.

"So," I asked her. "What's my latest prognosis?"

"Well," she said. "It comes down to this. You're dying."

"Not again," I said.

"Yup, Jimmy, you're still dying."

And we laughed, you know, because sometimes you'd rather cry.

"Well," the doctor said. "I've got other patients to see."

As she walked out, I wanted to call her back and make an urgent confession, to ask forgiveness, to offer truth in return for salvation. But she was only a doctor. A good doctor, but still just a doctor.

"Hey, Dr. Adams," I said.

"What?"

"Nothing," I said. "Just wanted to hear your name. It sounds like drums to these heavily medicated Indian ears of mine."

And she laughed and I laughed, too. That's what happened.

Norma was the world champion fry bread maker. Her fry bread was perfect, like one of those dreams you wake up from and say, *I didn't want to wake up.*

"I think this is your best fry bread ever," I told Norma one day. In fact, it was January 22.

"Thank you," she said. "Now you get to wash the dishes."

So I was washing the dishes when the phone rang. Norma answered it and I could hear her half of the conversation.

"Hello."

"Yes, this is Norma Many Horses."

"No."

"No!"

"*No!*" Norma yelled as she threw the phone down and ran outside. I picked the receiver up carefully, afraid of what it might say to me.

"Hello," I said.

"Who am I speaking to?" the voice on the other end asked.

"Jimmy Many Horses. I'm Norma's husband."

"Oh, Mr. Many Horses. I hate to be the bearer of bad news, but, uh, as I just told your wife, your mother-in-law, uh, passed away this morning."

"Thank you," I said, hung up the phone, and saw that Norma had returned.

"Oh, Jimmy," she said, talking through tears.

"I can't believe I just said *thank you* to that guy," I said. "What does that mean? Thank you that my mother-in-law is dead? Thank you that you told me that my mother-in-law is dead? Thank you that you told me that my mother-in-law is dead and made my wife cry?"

"Jimmy," Norma said. "Stop. It's not funny."

But I didn't stop. Then or now.

Still, you have to realize that laughter saved Norma and me from pain, too. Humor was an antiseptic that cleaned the deepest of personal wounds.

Once, a Washington State patrolman stopped Norma and me as we drove to Spokane to see a movie, get some dinner, a Big Gulp at 7-11.

"Excuse me, officer," I asked. "What did I do wrong?"

"You failed to make proper signal for a turn a few blocks back," he said.

That was interesting because I had been driving down a straight highway for over five miles. The only turns possible were down dirt roads toward houses where no one I ever knew had lived. But I knew to play along with his game. All you can hope for in these little wars is to minimize the amount of damage.

"I'm sorry about that, officer," I said. "But you know how it is. I was listening to the radio, tapping my foot. It's those drums, you know?"

"Whatever," the trooper said. "Now, I need your driver's license, registration, and proof of insurance."

I handed him the stuff and he barely looked at it. He leaned down into the window of the car.

"Hey, chief," he asked. "Have you been drinking?"

"I don't drink," I said.

"How about your woman there?"

"Ask her yourself," I said.

The trooper looked at me, blinked a few seconds, paused for dramatic effect, and said, "Don't you even think about telling me what I should do."

"I don't drink, either," Norma said quickly, hoping to avoid any further confrontation. "And I wasn't driving anyway."

"That don't make any difference," the trooper said. "Washington State has a new law against riding as a passenger in an Indian car."

"Officer," I said. "That ain't new. We've known about that one for a couple hundred years."

The trooper smiled a little, but it was a hard smile. You know the kind.

"However," he said. "I think we can make some kind of arrangement so none of this has to go on your record."

"How much is it going to cost me?" I asked.

"How much do you have?"

"About a hundred bucks."

"Well," the trooper said. "I don't want to leave you with nothing. Let's say the fine is ninety-nine dollars."

I gave him all the money, though, four twenties, a ten, eight dollar bills, and two hundred pennies in a sandwich bag.

"Hey," I said. "Take it all. That extra dollar is a tip, you know? Your service has been excellent."

Norma wanted to laugh then. She covered her mouth and pretended to cough. His face turned red. I mean redder than it already was.

"In fact," I said as I looked at the trooper's badge. "I might just send a letter to your commanding officer. I'll just write that Washington State Patrolman D. Nolan, badge number 13746, was polite, courteous, and above all, legal as an eagle."

Norma laughed out loud now.

"Listen," the trooper said. "I can just take you both in right now. For reckless driving, resisting arrest, threatening an officer with physical violence."

"If you do," Norma said and jumped into the fun, "I'll just tell everyone how respectful you were of our Native traditions, how much you understood about the social conditions that lead to the criminal acts of so many Indians. I'll say you were sympathetic, concerned, and intelligent."

"Fucking Indians," the trooper said as he threw the sandwich bag of pennies back into our car, sending them flying all over the interior. "And keep your damn change."

We watched him walk back to his cruiser, climb in, and drive off, breaking four or five laws as he flipped a U-turn, left

166

rubber, crossed the center line, broke the speed limit, and ran through a stop sign without lights and siren.

We laughed as we picked up the scattered pennies from the floor of the car. It was a good thing that the trooper threw that change back at us because we found just enough gas money to get us home.

After Norma left me, I'd occasionally get postcards from powwows all over the country. She missed me in Washington, Oregon, Idaho, Montana, Nevada, Utah, New Mexico, and California. I just stayed on the Spokane Indian Reservation and missed her from the doorway of my HUD house, from the living room window, waiting for the day that she would come back.

But that's how Norma operated. She told me once that she would leave me whenever the love started to go bad.

"I ain't going to watch the whole thing collapse," she said. "I'll get out when the getting is good."

"You wouldn't even try to save us?" I asked.

"It wouldn't be worth saving at that point."

"That's pretty cold."

"That's not cold," she said. "It's practical."

But don't get me wrong, either. Norma was a warrior in every sense of the word. She would drive a hundred miles round-trip to visit tribal elders in the nursing homes in Spokane. When one of those elders died, Norma would weep violently, throw books and furniture.

"Every one of our elders who dies takes a piece of our past away," she said. "And that hurts more because I don't know how much of a future we have."

And once, when we drove up on a really horrible car wreck, she held a dying man's head in her lap and sang to him until he passed away. He was a white guy, too. Remember that. She kept that memory so close to her that she had nightmares for a year.

"I always dream that it's you who's dying," she told me and didn't let me drive the car for almost a year.

Norma, she was always afraid; she wasn't afraid.

One thing that I noticed in the hospital as I coughed myself up and down the bed: A clock, at least one of those old-style clocks with hands and a face, looks just like somebody laughing if you stare at it long enough.

The hospital released me because they decided that I would be much more comfortable at home. And there I was, at home, writing letters to my loved ones on special reservation stationery that read: FROM THE DEATH BED OF JAMES MANY HORSES, III.

But in reality, I sat at my kitchen table to write, and DEATH TABLE just doesn't have the necessary music. I'm also the only James Many Horses, but there is a certain dignity to any kind of artificial tradition.

Anyway, I sat there at the death table, writing letters from my death bed, when there was a knock on the door.

"Come in," I yelled, knowing the door was locked, and smiled when it rattled against the frame.

"It's locked," a female voice said and it was a female voice I recognized.

"Norma?" I asked as I unlocked and opened the door.

She was beautiful. She had either gained or lost twenty pounds, one braid hung down a little longer than the other, and she had ironed her shirt until the creases were sharp.

"Honey," she said. "I'm home."

I was silent. That was a rare event.

"Honey," she said. "I've been gone so long and I missed you so much. But now I'm back. Where I belong."

I had to smile.

"Where are the kids?" she asked.

"They're asleep," I said, recovered just in time to continue the joke. "Poor little guys tried to stay awake, you know? They wanted to be up when you got home. But, one by one, they dropped off, fell asleep, and I had to carry them off into their little beds."

"Well," Norma said. "I'll just go in and kiss them quietly. Tell them how much I love them. Fix the sheets and blankets so they'll be warm all night."

She smiled.

"Jimmy," she said. "You look like shit."

"Yeah, I know."

"I'm sorry I left."

"Where've you been?" I asked, though I didn't really want to know.

"In Arlee. Lived with a Flathead cousin of mine."

"Cousin as in cousin? Or cousin as in I-was-fucking-him-but-don't-want-to-tell-you-because-you're-dying?"

169

She smiled even though she didn't want to.

"Well," she said. "I guess you'd call him more of that second kind of cousin."

Believe me: nothing ever hurt more. Not even my tumors which are the approximate size of baseballs.

"Why'd you come back?" I asked her.

She looked at me, tried to suppress a giggle, then broke out into full-fledged laughter. I joined her.

"Well," I asked her again after a while. "Why'd you come back?"

She turned stoic, gave me that beautiful Tonto face, and said, "Because he was so fucking serious about everything."

We laughed a little more and then I asked her one more time, "Really, why'd you come back?"

"Because someone needs to help you die the right way," she said. "And we both know that dying ain't something you ever done before."

I had to agree with that.

"And maybe," she said, "because making fry bread and helping people die are the last two things Indians are good at."

"Well," I said. "At least you're good at one of them."

And we laughed.

INDIAN EDUCATION

FIRST GRADE

My hair was too short and my U.S. Government glasses were horn-rimmed, ugly, and all that first winter in school, the other Indian boys chased me from one corner of the playground to the other. They pushed me down, buried me in the snow until I couldn't breathe, thought I'd never breathe again.

They stole my glasses and threw them over my head, around my outstretched hands, just beyond my reach, until someone tripped me and sent me falling again, facedown in the snow.

I was always falling down; my Indian name was Junior Falls Down. Sometimes it was Bloody Nose or Steal-His-Lunch. Once, it was Cries-Like-a-White-Boy, even though none of us had seen a white boy cry.

Then it was a Friday morning recess and Frenchy SiJohn threw snowballs at me while the rest of the Indian boys tortured some other *top-yogh-yaught* kid, another weakling. But Frenchy was confident enough to torment me all by himself, and most days I would have let him.

But the little warrior in me roared to life that day and knocked Frenchy to the ground, held his head against the snow, and punched him so hard that my knuckles and the snow made symmetrical bruises on his face. He almost looked like he was wearing war paint.

But he wasn't the warrior. I was. And I chanted *It's a good day to die, it's a good day to die*, all the way down to the principal's office.

SECOND GRADE

Betty Towle, missionary teacher, redheaded and so ugly that no one ever had a puppy crush on her, made me stay in for recess fourteen days straight.

"Tell me you're sorry," she said.

"Sorry for what?" I asked.

"Everything," she said and made me stand straight for

fifteen minutes, eagle-armed with books in each hand. One was a math book; the other was English. But all I learned was that gravity can be painful.

For Halloween I drew a picture of her riding a broom with a scrawny cat on the back. She said that her God would never forgive me for that.

Once, she gave the class a spelling test but set me aside and gave me a test designed for junior high students. When I spelled all the words right, she crumpled up the paper and made me eat it.

"You'll learn respect," she said.

She sent a letter home with me that told my parents to either cut my braids or keep me home from class. My parents came in the next day and dragged their braids across Betty Towle's desk.

"Indians, indians, indians." She said it without capitalization. She called me "indian, indian, indian."

And I said, *Yes, I am. I am Indian. Indian, I am.*

THIRD GRADE

My traditional Native American art career began and ended with my very first portrait: *Stick Indian Taking a Piss in My Backyard.*

As I circulated the original print around the classroom, Mrs. Schluter intercepted and confiscated my art.

Censorship, I might cry now. *Freedom of expression,* I would write in editorials to the tribal newspaper.

In third grade, though, I stood alone in the corner, faced the wall, and waited for the punishment to end.

I'm still waiting.

FOURTH GRADE

"You should be a doctor when you grow up," Mr. Schluter told me, even though his wife, the third grade teacher, thought I was crazy beyond my years. My eyes always looked like I had just hit-and-run someone.

"Guilty," she said. "You always look guilty."

"Why should I be a doctor?" I asked Mr. Schluter.

"So you can come back and help the tribe. So you can heal people."

That was the year my father drank a gallon of vodka a day and the same year that my mother started two hundred different quilts but never finished any. They sat in separate, dark places in our HUD house and wept savagely.

I ran home after school, heard their Indian tears, and looked in the mirror. *Doctor Victor,* I called myself, invented an education, talked to my reflection. *Doctor Victor to the emergency room.*

FIFTH GRADE

I picked up a basketball for the first time and made my first shot. No. I missed my first shot, missed the basket completely, and the ball landed in the dirt and sawdust, sat there just like I had sat there only minutes before.

174

But it felt good, that ball in my hands, all those possibilities and angles. It was mathematics, geometry. It was beautiful.

At that same moment, my cousin Steven Ford sniffed rubber cement from a paper bag and leaned back on the merry-go-round. His ears rang, his mouth was dry, and everyone seemed so far away.

But it felt good, that buzz in his head, all those colors and noises. It was chemistry, biology. It was beautiful.

Oh, do you remember those sweet, almost innocent choices that the Indian boys were forced to make?

SIXTH GRADE

Randy, the new Indian kid from the white town of Springdale, got into a fight an hour after he first walked into the reservation school.

Stevie Flett called him out, called him a squawman, called him a pussy, and called him a punk.

Randy and Stevie, and the rest of the Indian boys, walked out into the playground.

"Throw the first punch," Stevie said as they squared off.

"No," Randy said.

"Throw the first punch," Stevie said again.

"No," Randy said again.

"Throw the first punch!" Stevie said for the third time,

and Randy reared back and pitched a knuckle fastball that broke Stevie's nose.

We all stood there in silence, in awe.

That was Randy, my soon-to-be first and best friend, who taught me the most valuable lesson about living in the white world: *Always throw the first punch.*

SEVENTH GRADE

I leaned through the basement window of the HUD house and kissed the white girl who would later be raped by her foster-parent father, who was also white. They both lived on the reservation, though, and when the headlines and stories filled the papers later, not one word was made of their color.

Just Indians being Indians, someone must have said somewhere and they were wrong.

But on the day I leaned through the basement window of the HUD house and kissed the white girl, I felt the good-byes I was saying to my entire tribe. I held my lips tight against her lips, a dry, clumsy, and ultimately stupid kiss.

But I was saying good-bye to my tribe, to all the Indian girls and women I might have loved, to all the Indian men who might have called me cousin, even brother.

I kissed that white girl and when I opened my eyes, she was gone from the reservation, and when I opened my eyes, I was gone from the reservation, living in a farm town where a beautiful white girl asked my name.

"Junior Polatkin," I said, and she laughed.

After that, no one spoke to me for another five hundred years.

EIGHTH GRADE

At the farm town junior high, in the boys' bathroom, I could hear voices from the girls' bathroom, nervous whispers of anorexia and bulimia. I could hear the white girls' forced vomiting, a sound so familiar and natural to me after years of listening to my father's hangovers.

"Give me your lunch if you're just going to throw it up," I said to one of those girls once.

I sat back and watched them grow skinny from self-pity.

Back on the reservation, my mother stood in line to get us commodities. We carried them home, happy to have food, and opened the canned beef that even the dogs wouldn't eat.

But we ate it day after day and grew skinny from self-pity.

There is more than one way to starve.

NINTH GRADE

At the farm town high school dance, after a basketball game in an overheated gym where I had scored twenty-seven points and pulled down thirteen rebounds, I passed out during a slow song.

As my white friends revived me and prepared to take me to the emergency room where doctors would later diagnose my diabetes, the Chicano teacher ran up to us.

"Hey," he said. "What's that boy been drinking? I know all about these Indian kids. They start drinking real young."

Sharing dark skin doesn't necessarily make two men brothers.

TENTH GRADE

I passed the written test easily and nearly flunked the driving, but still received my Washington State driver's license on the same day that Wally Jim killed himself by driving his car into a pine tree.

No traces of alcohol in his blood, good job, wife and two kids.

"Why'd he do it?" asked a white Washington State trooper.

All the Indians shrugged their shoulders, looked down at the ground.

"Don't know," we all said, but when we look in the mirror, see the history of our tribe in our eyes, taste failure in the tap water, and shake with old tears, we understand completely.

Believe me, everything looks like a noose if you stare at it long enough.

ELEVENTH GRADE

Last night I missed two free throws which would have won the game against the best team in the state. The farm town high school I play for is nicknamed the "Indians," and I'm probably the only actual Indian ever to play for a team with such a mascot.

This morning I pick up the sports page and read the headline: INDIANS LOSE AGAIN.

Go ahead and tell me none of this is supposed to hurt me very much.

TWELFTH GRADE

I walk down the aisle, valedictorian of this farm town high school, and my cap doesn't fit because I've grown my hair longer than it's ever been. Later, I stand as the school board chairman recites my awards, accomplishments, and scholarships.

I try to remain stoic for the photographers as I look toward the future.

Back home on the reservation, my former classmates graduate: a few can't read, one or two are just given attendance diplomas, most look forward to the parties. The bright students are shaken, frightened, because they don't know what comes next.

They smile for the photographer as they look back toward tradition.

The tribal newspaper runs my photograph and the photograph of my former classmates side by side.

POSTSCRIPT: CLASS REUNION

Victor said, "Why should we organize a reservation high school reunion? My graduating class has a reunion every weekend at the Powwow Tavern."

THE LONE RANGER AND TONTO FISTFIGHT IN HEAVEN

Too hot to sleep so I walked down to the Third Avenue 7-11 for a Creamsicle and the company of a graveyard-shift cashier. I know that game. I worked graveyard for a Seattle 7-11 and got robbed once too often. The last time the bastard locked me in the cooler. He even took my money and basketball shoes.

The graveyard-shift worker in the Third Avenue 7-11 looked like they all do. Acne scars and a bad haircut, work pants that showed off his white socks, and those cheap black shoes that have no support. My arches still ache from my year at the Seattle 7-11.

"Hello," he asked when I walked into his store. "How you doing?"

I gave him a half-wave as I headed back to the freezer. He looked me over so he could describe me to the police later. I knew the look. One of my old girlfriends said I started to look at her that way, too. She left me not long after that. No, I left her and don't blame her for anything. That's how it happened. When one person starts to look at another like a criminal, then the love is over. It's logical.

I don't trust you," she said to me. "You get too angry."

She was white and I lived with her in Seattle. Some nights we fought so bad that I would just get in my car and drive all night, only stop to fill up on gas. In fact, I worked the graveyard shift to spend as much time away from her as possible. But I learned all about Seattle that way, driving its back ways and dirty alleys.

Sometimes, though, I would forget where I was and get lost. I'd drive for hours, searching for something familiar. Seems like I'd spent my whole life that way, looking for anything I recognized. Once, I ended up in a nice residential neighborhood and somebody must have been worried because the police showed up and pulled me over.

"What are you doing out here?" the police officer asked me as he looked over my license and registration.

"I'm lost."

"Well, where are you supposed to be?" he asked me, and I knew there were plenty of places I wanted to be, but none where I was supposed to be.

182

"I got in a fight with my girlfriend," I said. "I was just driving around, blowing off steam, you know?"

"Well, you should be more careful where you drive," the officer said. "You're making people nervous. You don't fit the profile of the neighborhood."

I wanted to tell him that I didn't really fit the profile of the country but I knew it would just get me into trouble.

"Can I help you?" the 7-11 clerk asked me loudly, searching for some response that would reassure him that I wasn't an armed robber. He knew this dark skin and long, black hair of mine was dangerous. I had potential.

"Just getting a Creamsicle," I said after a long interval. It was a sick twist to pull on the guy, but it was late and I was bored. I grabbed my Creamsicle and walked back to the counter slowly, scanned the aisles for effect. I wanted to whistle low and menacingly but I never learned to whistle.

"Pretty hot out tonight?" he asked, that old rhetorical weather bullshit question designed to put us both at ease.

"Hot enough to make you go crazy," I said and smiled. He swallowed hard like a white man does in those situations. I looked him over. Same old green, red, and white 7-11 jacket and thick glasses. But he wasn't ugly, just misplaced and marked by loneliness. If he wasn't working there that night, he'd be at home alone, flipping through channels and wishing he could afford HBO or Showtime.

"Will this be all?" he asked me, in that company effort to make me do some impulse shopping. Like adding a clause onto a treaty. *We'll take Washington and Oregon and you get six pine trees and a brand-new Chrysler Cordoba.* I knew how to make and break promises.

"No," I said and paused. "Give me a Cherry Slushie, too."

"What size?" he asked, relieved.

"Large," I said, and he turned his back to me to make the drink. He realized his mistake but it was too late. He stiffened, ready for the gunshot or the blow behind the ear. When it didn't come, he turned back to me.

"I'm sorry," he said. "What size did you say?"

"Small," I said and changed the story.

"But I thought you said large."

"If you knew I wanted a large, then why did you ask me again?" I asked him and laughed. He looked at me, couldn't decide if I was giving him serious shit or just goofing. There was something about him I liked, even if it was three in the morning and he was white.

"Hey," I said. "Forget the Slushie. What I want to know is if you know all the words to the theme from 'The Brady Bunch'?"

He looked at me, confused at first, then laughed.

"Shit," he said. "I was hoping you weren't crazy. You were scaring me."

"Well, I'm going to get crazy if you don't know the words."

He laughed loudly then, told me to take the Creamsicle for free. He was the graveyard-shift manager and those little demonstrations of power tickled him. All seventy-five cents of it. I knew how much everything cost.

"Thanks," I said to him and walked out the door. I took

my time walking home, let the heat of the night melt the Cream-sicle all over my hand. At three in the morning I could act just as young as I wanted to act. There was no one around to ask me to grow up.

In Seattle, I broke lamps. She and I would argue and I'd break a lamp, just pick it up and throw it down. At first she'd buy replacement lamps, expensive and beautiful. But after a while she'd buy lamps from Goodwill or garage sales. Then she just gave up the idea entirely and we'd argue in the dark.

"You're just like your brother," she'd yell. "Drunk all the time and stupid."

"My brother don't drink that much."

She and I never tried to hurt each other physically. I did love her, after all, and she loved me. But those arguments were just as damaging as a fist. Words can be like that, you know? When-ever I get into arguments now, I remember her and I also remem-ber Muhammad Ali. He knew the power of his fists but, more importantly, he knew the power of his words, too. Even though he only had an IQ of 80 or so, Ali was a genius. And she was a genius, too. She knew exactly what to say to cause me the most pain.

But don't get me wrong. I walked through that relation-ship with an executioner's hood. Or more appropriately, with war paint and sharp arrows. She was a kindergarten teacher and I continually insulted her for that.

"Hey, schoolmarm," I asked. "Did your kids teach you anything new today?"

And I always had crazy dreams. I always have had them, but it seemed they became nightmares more often in Seattle.

In one dream, she was a missionary's wife and I was a minor war chief. We fell in love and tried to keep it secret. But the missionary caught us fucking in the barn and shot me. As I lay dying, my tribe learned of the shooting and attacked the whites all across the reservation. I died and my soul drifted above the reservation.

Disembodied, I could see everything that was happening. Whites killing Indians and Indians killing whites. At first it was small, just my tribe and the few whites who lived there. But my dream grew, intensified. Other tribes arrived on horseback to continue the slaughter of whites, and the United States Cavalry rode into battle.

The most vivid image of that dream stays with me. Three mounted soldiers played polo with a dead Indian woman's head. When I first dreamed it, I thought it was just a product of my anger and imagination. But since then, I've read similar accounts of that kind of evil in the old West. Even more terrifying, though, is the fact that those kinds of brutal things are happening today in places like El Salvador.

All I know for sure, though, is that I woke from that dream in terror, packed up all my possessions, and left Seattle in the middle of the night.

"I love you," she said as I left her. "And don't ever come back."

I drove through the night, over the Cascades, down into the plains of central Washington, and back home to the Spokane Indian Reservation.

*　*　*

When I finished the Creamsicle that the 7-11 clerk gave me, I held the wooden stick up into the air and shouted out very loudly. A couple lights flashed on in windows and a police car cruised by me a few minutes later. I waved to the men in blue and they waved back accidentally. When I got home it was still too hot to sleep so I picked up a week-old newspaper from the floor and read.

There was another civil war, another terrorist bomb exploded, and one more plane crashed and all aboard were presumed dead. The crime rate was rising in every city with populations larger than 100,000, and a farmer in Iowa shot his banker after foreclosure on his 1,000 acres.

A kid from Spokane won the local spelling bee by spelling the word *rhinoceros*.

When I got back to the reservation, my family wasn't surprised to see me. They'd been expecting me back since the day I left for Seattle. There's an old Indian poet who said that Indians can reside in the city, but they can never live there. That's as close to truth as any of us can get.

Mostly I watched television. For weeks I flipped through channels, searched for answers in the game shows and soap operas. My mother would circle the want ads in red and hand the paper to me.

"What are you going to do with the rest of your life?" she asked.

"Don't know," I said, and normally, for almost any other Indian in the country, that would have been a perfectly fine

187

answer. But I was special, a former college student, a smart kid. I was one of those Indians who was supposed to make it, to rise above the rest of the reservation like a fucking eagle or something. I was the new kind of warrior.

For a few months I didn't even look at the want ads my mother circled, just left the newspaper where she had set it down. After a while, though, I got tired of television and started to play basketball again. I'd been a good player in high school, nearly great, and almost played at the college I attended for a couple years. But I'd been too out of shape from drinking and sadness to ever be good again. Still, I liked the way the ball felt in my hands and the way my feet felt inside my shoes.

At first I just shot baskets by myself. It was selfish, and I also wanted to learn the game again before I played against anybody else. Since I had been good before and embarrassed fellow tribal members, I knew they would want to take revenge on me. Forget about the cowboys versus Indians business. The most intense competition on any reservation is Indians versus Indians.

But on the night I was ready to play for real, there was this white guy at the gym, playing with all the Indians.

"Who is that?" I asked Jimmy Seyler.

"He's the new BIA chief's kid."

"Can he play?"

"Oh, yeah."

And he could play. He played Indian ball, fast and loose, better than all the Indians there.

"How long's he been playing here?" I asked.

"Long enough."

I stretched my muscles, and everybody watched me. All

these Indians watched one of their old and dusty heroes. Even though I had played most of my ball at the white high school I went to, I was still all Indian, you know? I was Indian when it counted, and this BIA kid needed to be beaten by an Indian, any Indian.

I jumped into the game and played well for a little while. It felt good. I hit a few shots, grabbed a rebound or two, played enough defense to keep the other team honest. Then that white kid took over the game. He was too good. Later, he'd play college ball back East and would nearly make the Knicks team a couple years on. But we didn't know any of that would happen. We just knew he was better that day and every other day.

The next morning I woke up tired and hungry, so I grabbed the want ads, found a job I wanted, and drove to Spokane to get it. I've been working at the high school exchange program ever since, typing and answering phones. Sometimes I wonder if the people on the other end of the line know that I'm Indian and if their voices would change if they did know.

One day I picked up the phone and it was her, calling from Seattle.

"I got your number from your mom," she said. "I'm glad you're working."

"Yeah, nothing like a regular paycheck."

"Are you drinking?"

"No, I've been on the wagon for almost a year."

"Good."

The connection was good. I could hear her breathing in the spaces between our words. How do you talk to the real person whose ghost has haunted you? How do you tell the difference between the two?

"Listen," I said. "I'm sorry for everything."

"Me, too."

"What's going to happen to us?" I asked her and wished I had the answer for myself.

"I don't know," she said. "I want to change the world."

These days, living alone in Spokane, I wish I lived closer to the river, to the falls where ghosts of salmon jump. I wish I could sleep. I put down my paper or book and turn off all the lights, lie quietly in the dark. It may take hours, even years, for me to sleep again. There's nothing surprising or disappointing in that.

I know how all my dreams end anyway.

FAMILY PORTRAIT

The television was always loud, too loud, until every
conversation was distorted, fragmented.

"Dinner" sounded like "Leave me alone."

"I love you" sounded like "Inertia."

"Please" sounded like "Sacrifice."

Believe me, the television was always too loud. At three
in the morning I woke from ordinary nightmares to hear the
television pounding the ceiling above my bed. Sometimes it was
just white noise, the end of another broadcasting day. Other
times it was a bad movie made worse by the late hour and
interrupted sleep.

"Drop your weapons and come out with your hands above your head" sounded too much like "Trust me, the world is yours."

"The aliens are coming! The aliens are coming!" sounded too much like "Just one more beer, sweetheart, and then we'll go home."

"Junior, I lost the money" sounded too much like "You'll never have a dream come true."

I don't know where all the years went. I remember only the television in detail. All the other moments worth remembering became stories that changed with each telling, until nothing was aboriginal or recognizable.

For instance, in the summer of 1972 or 1973 or only in our minds, the reservation disappeared. I remember standing on the front porch of our HUD house, practicing on my plastic saxophone, when the reservation disappeared.

Finally, I remember thinking, but I was six years old, or seven. I don't know for sure how old; I was Indian.

Just like that, there was nothing there beyond the bottom step. My older brother told me he'd give me a quarter if I jumped into the unknown. My twin sisters cried equal tears; their bicycles had been parked out by the pine trees, all of it vanished.

My mother came out to investigate the noise. She stared out past the bottom step for a long time, but there was no expression on her face when she went back to wash the potatoes.

My father was happily drunk and he stumbled off the bottom step before any of us could stop him. He came back years later with diabetes and a pocketful of quarters. The seeds in the cuffs of his pants dropped to the floor of our house and grew into orange trees.

"Nothing is possible without Vitamin C," my mother told us, but I knew she meant to say, "Don't want everything so much."

Often the stories contain people who never existed before our collective imaginations created them.

My brother and I remember our sisters scraped all the food that dropped off our plates during dinner into a pile in the center of the table. Then they placed their teeth against the edge of the table and scraped all the food into their open mouths.

Our parents don't remember that happening, and our sisters cry out, "No, no, we were never that hungry!"

Still, my brother and I cannot deny the truth of our story. We were there. Maybe hunger informs our lives.

My family tells me stories of myself, small events and catastrophic diseases I don't remember but accept as the beginning of my story.

After surgery to relieve fluid pressure on my brain, I started to dance.

"No," my mother tells me. "You had epileptic seizures."

"No," my father tells her. "He was dancing."

During "The Tonight Show" I pretended sleep on the couch while my father sat in his chair and watched the television.

"It was Doc's trumpet that made you dance," my father told me.

"No, it was grand mal seizures punctuated by moments of extreme perception," my mother told him.

She wanted to believe I could see the future. She secretly knew the doctors had inserted another organ into my skull, transplanted a twentieth-century vision.

One winter she threw me outside in my underwear and refused to let me back into the house until I answered her questions.

"Will my children love me when I'm old?" she asked, but I knew she wanted to ask me, "Will I regret my life?"

Then there was music, scratched 45's and eight-track tapes. We turned the volume too high for the speakers, until the music was tinny and distorted. But we danced, until my oldest sister tore her only pair of nylons and wept violently. But we danced, until we shook dust down from the ceiling and chased bats out of the attic into the daylight. But we danced, in our mismatched clothes and broken shoes. I wrote my name in Magic Marker on my shoes, my first name on the left toe and my last name on the right toe, with my true name somewhere in between. But we danced, with empty stomachs and nothing for dinner except sleep. All night we lay awake with sweat on our backs and blisters on our soles. All night we fought waking nightmares until sleep came with nightmares of its own. I re-member the nightmare about the thin man in a big hat who took the Indian children away from their parents. He came with scissors to cut hair and a locked box to hide all the am-putated braids. But we danced, under wigs and between un-

194

finished walls, through broken promises and around empty cupboards.

It was a dance.

Still, we can be surprised.

My sister told me she could recognize me by the smell of my clothes. She said she could close her eyes and pick me out of a crowd by just the smell of my shirt.

I knew she meant to say *I love you*.

With all the systems of measurements we had available, I remember the degree of sunlight most. It was there continuously, winter or summer. The cold came by accident, the sun by design.

Then there was the summer of sniffing gas. My sisters bent their heads at impossible angles to reach the gas tanks of BIA vehicles. Everything so bright and precise, it hurt the brain. Eardrums pounded by the slightest noise; a dog barking could change the shape of the earth.

I remember my brother stretched out over the lawnmower, his mouth pressed tightly to the mouth of the gas tank. It was a strange kiss, his first kiss, his lips burnt and clothes flammable. He tried to dance away, he named every blade of grass he crushed when he fell on his ass. Everything under water, like walking across the bottom of Benjamin Lake, past dead horses and abandoned tires. Legs tangled in seaweed, dance, dance again, kick the feet until you break free. Stare up at the surface, sunlight filtered through water like fingers, like a hand filled with the promise of love and oxygen.

WARNING: *Intentional misuse by deliberately concentrating and inhaling the contents can be harmful or fatal.*

How much do we remember of what hurts us most? I've been thinking about pain, how each of us constructs our past to justify what we feel now. How each successive pain distorts the preceding. Let's say I remember sunlight as a measurement of this story, how it changed the shape of the family portrait. My father shields his eyes and makes his face a shadow. He could be anyone then, but my eyes are closed in the photo. I cannot remember what I was thinking. Maybe I wanted to stand, stretch my legs, raise my arms above my head, open my mouth wide, and fill my lungs. *Breathe, breathe.* Maybe my hair is so black it collects all the available light.

Suddenly it is winter and I'm trying to start the car.

"Give it more gas," my father shouts from the house.

I put my foot to the fire wall, feel the engine shudder in response. My hands grip the steering wheel tightly. They are not mine this morning. These hands are too strong, too necessary for even the smallest gestures. I can make fists and throw my anger into walls and plasterboard. I can pick up a toothbrush or a pistol, touch the face of a woman I love. Years ago, these hands might have held the spear that held the salmon that held the dream of the tribe. Years ago, these hands might have touched the hands of the dark-skinned men who touched medicine and the magic of ordinary gods. Now, I put my hand to gearshift, my heart to the cold wind.

"Give it more gas," my father yells.

I put the car into Drive and then I am gone, down the road, carefully, touching the brake like I touch my dreams. Once, my father and I drove this same road and he told the story of the first television he ever saw.

"The television was in the window of a store in Coeur d'Alene. Me and all the guys would walk down there and watch it. Just one channel and all it showed was a woman sitting on top of a television that showed the same woman sitting on top of the same television. Over and over until it hurt your eyes and head. That's the way I remember it. And she was always singing some song. I think it was 'A Girl on Top of the World.' "

This is how we find our history, how we sketch our family portrait, how we snap the photograph at the precise moment when someone's mouth is open and ready to ask a question. *How?*

There is a girl on top of the world. She is owldancing with my father. That is the story by which we measure all our stories, until we understand that one story can never be all.

There is a girl on top of the world. She is singing the blues. That is the story by which we measure heartbreak. Maybe she is my sister or my other sister or my oldest sister dead in the house fire. Maybe she is my mother with her hands in the fry bread. Maybe she is my brother.

There is a girl on top of the world. She is telling us her story. That is the story by which we measure the beginning of all of our lives. *Listen, listen, what can be calling?* She is why we hold

197

each other tight; she is why our fear refuses naming. She is the fancydancer; she is forgiveness.

The television was always loud, too loud, until every emotion was measured by the half hour. We hid our faces behind masks that suggested other histories; we touched hands accidentally and our skin sparked like a personal revolution. We stared across the room at each other, waited for the conversation and the conversion, watched wasps and flies battering against the windows. We were children; we were open mouths. Open in hunger, in anger, in laughter, in prayer.

Jesus, we all want to survive.

SOMEBODY KEPT SAYING

POWWOW

I knew Norma before she ever met her husband-to-be, James Many Horses. I knew her back when there was good fry bread to be eaten at the powwow, before the old women died and took their recipes with them. That's how it's going. Sometimes it feels like our tribe is dying a piece of bread at a time. But Norma, she was always trying to save it, she was a cultural lifeguard, watching out for those of us that were so close to drowning.

She was really young, too, not all that much older than me, but everybody called her grandmother anyway, as a sign of respect.

"Hey, grandmother," I said when she walked by me as I sat at another terrible fry bread stand.

"Hi, Junior," she said and walked over to me. She shook my hand, loosely, like Indians do, using only her fingers. Not like those tight grips that white people use to prove something. She touched my hand like she was glad to see me, not like she wanted to break bones.

"Are you dancing this year?" I asked.

"Of course. Haven't you been down to the dance hall?"

"Not yet."

"Well, you should go watch the dancing. It's important."

We talked for a while longer, told some stories, and then she went on about her powwow agenda. Everybody wanted to talk to Norma, to share some time with her. I just liked to sit with her, put my reservation antennas up and adjust my reception. Didn't you know that Indians are born with two antennas that rise up and field emotional signals? Norma always said that Indians are the most sensitive people on the planet. For that matter, Indians are more sensitive than animals, too. We don't just watch things happen. Watching automatically makes the watcher part of the happening. That's what Norma taught me.

"Everything matters," she said. "Even the little things."

But it was more than just some bullshit Native religion, some fodder for the crystal-happy. Norma lived her life like we should all do. She didn't drink or smoke. But she could spend a night in the Powwow Tavern and dance hard. She could dance Indian and white. And that's a mean feat, since the two methods of dancing are mutually exclusive. I've seen Indians who are champion fancydancers trip all over themselves when Paula

200

Abdul is on the jukebox in the bar. And I've seen Indians who could do all this MTV Club dancing, electric slides and shit, all over the place and then look like a white person stumbling through the sawdust of a powwow.

One night I was in the Powwow Tavern and Norma asked me to dance. I'd never danced with her before, hadn't really danced much at all, Indian or white.

"Move your ass," she said. "This ain't Browning, Montana. It's Las Vegas."

So I moved my ass, shook my skinny brown butt until the whole bar was laughing, which was good. Even if I was the one being laughed at. And Norma and I laughed all night long and danced together all night long. Most nights, before James Many Horses showed up, Norma would dance with everybody, not choosing any favorites. She was a diplomat. But she only danced with me that night. Believe me, it was an honor. After the bar closed, she even drove me home since everybody else was headed to parties and I wanted to go to sleep.

"Hey," she said on the way home. "You can't dance very good but you got the heart of a dancer."

"Heart of the dancer," I said. "And feet like the buffalo."

And we laughed.

She dropped me at home, gave me a good night hug, and then drove on to her own HUD house. I went into my house and dreamed about her. Not like you think. I dreamed her a hundred years ago, riding bareback down on Little Falls Flats. Her hair was unbraided and she was yelling something to me as she rode closer to where I stood. I couldn't understand what she was saying, though. But it was a dream and I listen to my dreams.

"I dreamed about you the other night," I said to Norma the next time I saw her. I told her about the dream.

"I don't know what that means," she said. "I hope it's nothing bad."

"Maybe it just means I have a crush on you."

"No way," she said and laughed. "I've seen you hanging around with that Nadine Moses woman. You must have been dreaming about her."

"Nadine don't know how to ride a horse," I said.

"Who said anything about horses?" Norma said, and we both laughed for a good long time.

Norma could ride horses like she did live one hundred years ago. She was a rodeo queen, but not one of those rhinestone women. She was a roper, a breaker of wild ponies. She wrestled steers down to the ground and did that goofy old three-legged knot dance. Norma just wasn't quite as fast as some of the other Indian cowboys, though. I think, in the end, she was just having a good time. She'd hang with the cowboys and they'd sing songs for her, 49er songs that echoed beyond the evening's last campfire.

> Norma, I want to marry you
> Norma, I want to make you mine
> And we'll go dancing, dancing, dancing
> until the sun starts to shine.
> Way yah hi yo, Way yah hi yo!

Some nights Norma took an Indian cowboy or a cowboy Indian back to her tipi. And that was good. Some people would have you believe it's wrong, but it was two people sharing some body medicine. It wasn't like Norma was out snagging for men all the time. Most nights she just went home alone and sang herself to sleep.

Some people said that Norma took a woman home with her once in a while, too. Years ago, homosexuals were given special status within the tribe. They had powerful medicine. I think it's even more true today, even though our tribe has assimilated into homophobia. I mean, a person has to have magic to assert their identity without regard to all the bullshit, right?

Anyhow, or as we say around here, anyhoo, Norma held on to her status within the tribe despite all the rumors, the stories, the lies and jealous gossip. Even after she married that James Many Horses, who told so many jokes that he even made other Indians get tired of his joking.

The funny thing is that I always thought Norma would end up marrying Victor since she was so good at saving people and Victor needed more saving than most anybody besides Lester FallsApart. But she and Victor never got along, much. Victor was kind of a bully in his younger days, and I don't think Norma ever forgave him. I doubt Victor ever forgave herself for it. I think he said *I'm sorry* more than any other human being alive.

I remember once when Norma and I were sitting in the Powwow Tavern and Victor walked in, drunker than drunk.

"Where's the powwow?" Victor yelled.

"You're in the Powwow," somebody yelled back.

"No, I don't mean this goddamn bar. I mean, where's the powwow?"

"In your pants," somebody else yelled and we all laughed.

Victor staggered up to our table.

"Junior," he asked. "Where's the powwow?"

"There ain't no powwow going on," I said.

"Well," Victor said. "Somebody out in the parking lot kept saying powwow. And you know I love a good goddamn powwow."

"We all love a good powwow," Norma said.

Victor smiled a drunk smile at her, one of those smiles only possible through intoxication. The lips fall at odd angles, the left side of the face is slightly paralyzed, and skin shines with alcohol sweat. Nothing remotely approaching beauty.

"I'm going to go find the goddamn powwow," Victor said then and staggered out the door. He's on the wagon now but he used to get so drunk.

"Good luck," Norma said. That's one of the strangest things about the tribal ties that still exists. A sober Indian has infinite patience with a drunk Indian, even most of the Indians who have completely quit drinking. There ain't many who do stay sober. Most spend time in Alcoholics Anonymous meetings, and everybody gets to know the routines and use them on all occasions, not just at A.A. meetings.

"Hi, my name is Junior," I usually say when I walk into a bar or party where Indians have congregated.

"Hi, Junior," all the others shout in an ironic unison.

A few of the really smart-asses about the whole A.A. thing carry around little medals indicating how long they've been continuously drunk.

"Hi, my name is Lester FallsApart, and I've been drunk for twenty-seven straight years."

Norma didn't much go for that kind of humor, though. She laughed when it was funny but she didn't start anything up. Norma, she knew all about Indian belly laughter, the kind of laughter that made Indians squeeze their eyes up so tight they looked Chinese. Maybe that's where those rumors about crossing the Bering Bridge started. Maybe some of us Indians just laughed our way over to China 25,000 years ago and jumpstarted that civilization. But whenever I started in on my crazy theories, Norma would put her finger to my lips really gently.

"Junior," she would say with gentleness and patience. "Shut the fuck up."

Norma always was a genius with words. She used to write stories for the tribal newspaper. She was even their sports reporter for a while. I still got the news clipping of a story she wrote about the basketball game I won back in high school. In fact, I keep it tucked in my wallet and if I get drunk enough, I'll pull it out and read from it aloud, like it was a goddamn poem or something. But the way Norma wrote, I guess it was something close to a poem:

Junior's Jumpshot Just Enough for Redskin Win

With three seconds left on the clock last Saturday night and the Springdale Chargers in possession of the ball, it looked like even the Wellpinit Redskins might have to call in the United States Cavalry to help them win the first game of this just-a-baby basketball season.

But Junior Polatkin tipi-creeped the Chargers

by stealing the inbounds pass and then stealing the game away when he hit a three-thousand-foot jumper at the buzzer.

"I doubt we'll be filing any charges against Junior for theft," Tribal Chief of Police David WalksAlong said. "This was certainly a case of self-defense."

People were gossiping all around the rez about Junior's true identity.

"I think he was Crazy Horse for just a second," said an anonymous and maybe-just-a-little-crazy-themselves source.

This reporter thinks Junior happened to be a little lucky so his new Indian name will be Lucky Shot. Still, luck or not, Junior has earned a couple points more on the Warrior Scale.

Whenever I pull that clipping out with Norma around, she always threatens to tear it up. But she never does. She's proud of it, I can tell. I'd be proud, too. I mean, I'm proud I won that game. It was the only game we won that year. In fact, it was the only game the Wellpinit Redskins won in three years. It wasn't like we had bad teams. We always had two or three of the best players in the league, but winning wasn't always as important as getting drunk after the game for some and for going to the winter powwows for others. Some games, we'd only have five players.

I always wished we could have suited Norma up. She was taller than all of us and a better player than most of us. I don't really remember her playing in high school, but people say she could have played college ball if she would've gone to college. Same old story. But the reservation people who say things like that have never been off the reservation.

"What's it like out there?" Norma asked me when I came back from college, from the city, from cable television and delivered pizza.

"It's like a bad dream you never wake up from," I said, and it's true. Sometimes I still feel like half of me is lost in the city, with its foot wedged into a steam grate or something. Stuck in one of those revolving doors, going round and round while all the white people are laughing. Standing completely still on an escalator that will not move, but I didn't have the courage to climb the stairs by myself. Stuck in an elevator between floors with a white woman who keeps wanting to touch my hair.

There are some things that Indians would've never invented if given the chance.

"But the city gave you a son," Norma said, and that was true enough. Sometimes, though, it felt like half a son because the city had him during the week and every other weekend. The reservation only got him for six days a month. Visitation rights. That's how the court defined them. Visitation rights.

"Do you ever want kids?" I asked Norma.

"Yeah, of course," she said. "I want a dozen. I want my own tribe."

"You're kidding."

"Kind of. Don't know if I want to raise kids in this world. It's getting uglier by the second. And not just on the reservation."

"I know what you mean," I said. "You see where two people got shot in the bus station in Spokane last week? In Spokane! It's getting to be like New York City."

"New York City enough."

Norma was the kind of person who made you honest. She was so completely honest herself that you couldn't help it. Pretty soon I'd be telling her all my secrets, the bad and good.

"What's the worst thing you ever did?" she asked me.

"Probably that time I watched Victor beat the shit out of Thomas Builds-the-Fire."

"I remember that. I'm the one who broke it up. But you were just a kid. Must be something worse than that."

I thought about it awhile, but it didn't take me long to figure out what the worst thing I ever did was.

It was at a basketball game when I was in college. I was with a bunch of guys from my dormitory, all white guys, and we were drunk, really drunk. The other team had this player who just got out of prison. I mean, this guy was about twenty-eight and had a tough life. Grew up in inner-city Los Angeles and finally made it out, made it to college and was playing and studying hard. If you think about it, he and I had a whole lot in common. Much more in common than I had with those white boys I was drunk with.

Anyway, when that player comes out, I don't even re-member his name or maybe I don't want to remember it, we all start chanting at him. Really awful shit. Hateful. We all had these big cards we made to look like those GET OUT OF JAIL FREE cards in Monopoly. One guy was running around in a black-and-white convict shirt with a fake ball-and-chain. It was a really bad scene. The local newspaper had a big write-up. We even made it into a *People* Magazine article. It was about that player and how much he'd gone through and how he still had to fight so much ignorance and hate. When they asked him how it felt during that game where we all went crazy, he said, *It hurt.*

After I told Norma that story, she was quiet for a long time. A long time.

"If I drank," she said, "I would be getting drunk right about now because of that one."

"I've gotten drunk on it a few times."

"And if it still bothers you this much now," Norma said, "then think how bad that guy feels about it."

"I think about him all the time."

After I told Norma that story, she treated me differently for about a year. She wasn't mean or distant. Just different. But I understood. People can do things completely against their nature, completely. It's like some tiny earthquake comes roaring through your body and soul, and it's the only earthquake you'll ever feel. But it damages so much, cracks the foundations of your life forever.

So I just figured Norma wouldn't ever forgive me. She was like that. She was probably the most compassionate person on the reservation but she was also the most passionate. Then one day in the Trading Post she walked up to me and smiled.

"Pete Rose," she said.

"What?" I asked, completely confused.

"Pete Rose," she repeated.

"What?" I asked again, even more confused.

"That's your new Indian name," she said. "Pete Rose."

"Why?"

"Because you two got a whole lot in common."

"How?"

"Listen," Norma said. "Pete Rose played major league baseball in four different decades, has more hits than anybody in history. Hell, think about it. Going back to Little League and high school and all that, he's probably been smacking the ball around forever. Noah probably pitched him a few on the Ark. But after all that, all that greatness, he's only remembered for the bad stuff."

"Gambling," I said.

"That ain't right," she said.

"Not at all."

After that, Norma treated me the same as she did before she found out what I did in college. She made me try to find that basketball player, but I didn't have any luck. What would I have told him if I did find him? Would I just tell him that I was Pete Rose? Would he have understood that?

Then, on one strange, strange day when a plane had to emergency land on the reservation highway, and the cooler in the Trading Post broke down and they were giving away ice cream because it would've been wasted, and a bear fell asleep on the roof of the Catholic church, Norma ran up to me, nearly breathless.

"Pete Rose," she said. "They just voted to keep you out of the Hall of Fame. I'm sorry. But I still love you."

"Yeah, I know, Norma. I love you, too."

WITNESSES,
SECRET AND NOT

In 1979 I was just learning how to be thirteen. I didn't
know that I'd have to keep thinking about it until I
was twenty-five. I thought that once I figured out thirteen, then
it was history, junk for the archaeologists to find years later. I
thought it would keep working that way, figuring out each year
as it came, then discarding it when the new one came along. But
there's much more to the whole thing. I mean, I had to figure out
what it meant to be a boy, a man, too. Most of all, I had to find
out what it meant to be Indian, and there ain't no self-help
manuals for that last one.

And of course, I had to understand what it meant when my father got a phone call one night out on the reservation.

"Who's this?" my father asked when he picked the phone up. And it was the Secret Witness Program calling him from Spokane. Guess somebody turned my father's name in to the police. Said my father might know something about how Jerry Vincent disappeared about ten years earlier.

So we had to drive into Spokane the next day, and all the way I was asking him questions like I was the family police.

"What happened to Jerry Vincent?" I asked him.

"He just disappeared. Nobody knows for sure."

"If nobody knows what happened, then why do the police want to talk to you?"

"I was in the bar the night Jerry disappeared. Was partying a little bit with him. Guess that's why."

"Were you friends?"

"I guess. Yeah, we were friends. Mostly."

We drove that way, with me asking those questions, like how Jerry looked, how he talked, the way his clothes were wrinkled all the time. My father told me all those kind of things. About Jerry's wife, his kids. About being disappeared.

"He wasn't the first one to disappear like that. No way," my father said.

"Who else?" I asked.

"Just about everybody at one time or another. All those relocation programs sent reservation Indians to the cities, and sometimes they just got swallowed up. Happened to me. I didn't see or talk to anybody from home for a couple years."

"Not even Mom?"

"I didn't know her back then. Anyway, one day I come

hitchhiking back to the reservation and everybody tells me they heard I was dead, heard I'd disappeared. Just like that."

"Is that what happened to Jerry?"

"No, no. But I think everybody wanted it to be that way. Everybody wanted it that way because of the way it really happened."

"What do you mean?"

My father put both hands on the steering wheel. A good thing, too. Just then we went into a slide on the icy road. A mean slide, a 360-degree slide around the worst corner in the Reardan Canyon. Why is it that car accidents take so long to happen? And they seem to get slower as you grow older? I'd been in one accident or another every year of my life. Just after I was born, my mother ran a red light and was hit broadside. I got thrown out of the car and landed in an open dumpster. Ever since that, my life has been punctuated by more accidents, all ugly and lucky. And all so slow.

Anyway, there we were, my father and I, silent as hell while the car fancydanced across the ice. At age thirteen, nobody thinks they're going to die, so that wasn't my worry. But my father was forty-one and that's about the age that I figure a man starts to think about dying. Or starts to accept it as inevitable.

My father's hands never left the wheel and he stared straight ahead, as if the world outside the window wasn't completely revolving. He might as well have been watching television or a basketball game. It was happening. That's all my father allowed himself to think.

But we didn't wreck. Somehow the car turned completely around and we kept driving straight down the road as if the slide never took place. We didn't talk about it right afterward and we don't talk about it now. Does it exist? It's like that idiot question about the tree falling in the woods. I'm always asking myself if a near-accident is an accident, if standing right next to a disaster makes you part of the disaster or just a neighbor.

We just kept driving. And talking.

"What happened to Jerry Vincent?" I asked.

"He got shot in the head in the alley behind the bar and they buried his body up in Manito Park."

"Really? Do the police know that?"

"Yeah. I've told them quite a few times. I get called in about once a year, you know? And I always tell them the same thing. Yes, I was with Jerry that night. Yes, he was alive when I saw him last. Yeah, I know he was shot in the head in the alley behind the bar and they buried his body up in Manito Park somewhere. No, I don't know who shot him, I just know the story because every Indian knows the story. No, I don't know where the body is buried. No, I didn't shoot him or bury him. I just had a few beers with him that night. Had quite a few beers with him over the years. That's all."

"You got the whole thing memorized, don't you?"

"That's how it works."

We kept driving like that, driving that way, talking, asking questions, getting answers. It was snowing a little. The roads icy and dangerous.

From the reservation to Spokane is about an hour, through farming country, past Fairchild Air Force Base, and down into the valley. Because of the geography, Spokane has a lot of those air inversions, where this layer of filth hangs above the city and keeps everything trapped beneath it. The same bit of oxygen gets breathed over and over, passed through a hundred pair of lungs. It's pretty horrible, worse even than Los Angeles, I guess. On that day we drove into Spokane, the air was brown and I don't mean it looked brown. It was just brown, like breathing dirt directly. Like working in a coal mine.

"I've got mud in my mouth," I said.

"Me, too," my father said.

"It'd taste like this if I was buried alive, right?"

"I don't know. That's a pretty sick thought, enit?"

"Sick enough. What would it be like to die?"

"Don't know. Ain't ever died before."

"Must be kind of like disappearing," I said. "And you did disappear once."

"Maybe," my father said. "But disappearing ain't always so bad. I knew one guy who traveled to some islands way out in the Pacific and got trapped there for two years because of some weird tides. There were no telephones, no radios, no way of contacting anybody. Everyone back home thought he had died. The local newspaper even ran an obituary. Then one day he gets off the island, flies back home, and walks in the front door just like that."

"Really?"

"Really. And he said it was like starting over. Everybody was so goddamn happy to see him they forgot all about the bad things he did in the past. He said it was like being a newborn baby with everybody making funny noises in his face."

We drove through city streets, familiar with them all. We saw those Indians passed out in doorways, staggering down the sidewalk. We knew most of them by sight, half of them by name.

"Hey," my father said as we passed by an old Indian man. "That was Jimmy Shit Pants."

"Ain't seen him out on the reservation in a long time," I said.

"How long?"

"A long time."

We drove around the corner and came back to Jimmy. He wasn't quite drunk, a few sips from it actually. He had on a little red coat that couldn't have been warm enough for a Spokane winter. But he had some good boots. Probably got them from Goodwill or Salvation Army.

"Ya-hey, Jimmy," my father said. "Nice boots."

"Nice enough," Jimmy said.

"What's been going on?" my father asked.

"Not much."

"Been drinking too hard?"

"Hard enough."

"Hey, Jimmy," I asked. "Why haven't you been out on the reservation?"

"Don't know. You got five bucks I can borrow?"

I reached into my pocket and pulled out a dollar. It was all I had but I gave it up. Think about it this way. It was just a comic book and a Diet Pepsi for me. That ain't nothing compared to what it meant to Jimmy. My father gave Jimmy a few bucks, too. Just enough for a jug.

We drove off then and left Jimmy to make his own decisions. That's how it is. One Indian doesn't tell another what to do. We just watch things happen and then make comments. It's all about reaction as opposed to action.

"What time are you supposed to be at the police station?" I asked my father.

"About an hour."

"Want to get something to eat?"

"Yeah."

"How about a hamburger at Dick's?"

"Sounds good, enit?"

"Good enough."

So we drove on over to Dick's, the greasy fast-food place with extra-cheap hamburgers. We ordered what we always ordered: a Whammy burger, large fries, and a Big Buy Diet Pepsi. We order Diet since my father and I are both diabetic. Genetics, you know?

Sometimes it does feel like we are all defined by the food we eat, though. My father and I would be potted meat product, corned beef hash, fry bread, and hot chili. We would be potato chips, hot dogs, and fried bologna. We would be coffee with grounds sticking in our teeth.

Sometimes there was no food in the house. I called my father Hunger and he called me Pang. You know how that is, don't you?

Anyway, there we were, eating bad food and talking more stories.

"Hey," I asked my father. "If you knew who killed Jerry Vincent, would you tell the police?"

"Don't think so."

"Why not?"

"Because I don't think they care much anyway. Just make more trouble for Indians is all."

"Have you ever killed anyone?" I asked.

My father took a big drink of his Diet Pepsi, ate a few fries, bit into his burger. In that order. Then he took another bigger drink of his Diet Pepsi.

"Why do you want to know?" he asked.

"Don't know. Just curious, I guess."

"Well, I never killed anybody on purpose."

"You mean you killed somebody accidentally?"

"That's how it was."

"How do you kill somebody accidentally?"

"I got in a head-on wreck with another car. Killed the other driver. He was a white man."

"Did you go to jail?"

"No. I got lucky. He had alcohol in his blood."

"You mean he was drunk?" I asked.

"Yeah. And even though the wreck was mostly my fault, he got the blame. I was sober and the cops couldn't believe it. They'd never heard of a sober Indian getting in a car wreck."

"Like Ripley's Believe It or Not?"

"Something like that."

We finished our lunch and drove over to the police station. Spokane is a small city. That's all there is to say about that. We made it to the police station in a few minutes, even though my father drives very slowly. He drives that way because he's tired of accidents. Anyway, we pull into the parking lot and park. That's what you're supposed to do.

"Are you scared?" I asked my father.

"A little bit."

"Should I come with you?"

218

"No. Wait out here in the car."

I watched my father walk toward the police station. Wearing old jeans and a red T-shirt, he looked very obvious next to the police uniforms and three-piece suits. He looked as Indian as you can get. I could spend my whole life on the reservation and never once would I see a friend of mine and think how Indian he looked. But as soon as I get off the reservation, among all the white people, every Indian gets exaggerated. My father's braids looked three miles long and black and shiny as a police-issue revolver. He turned back and waved to me just before he disappeared into the station.

I imagined that he walked up to the receptionist and asked for directions.

"Excuse me," he might have said. "I have an appointment with Detective Moore."

"Detective Moore is out," she said.

"Well," my father said. "How about Detective Clayton?"

"Let me check."

I imagined that the receptionist led my father back to the detective's desk, sat him down, and gave him that look reserved for criminals and pizza delivery men. You know exactly what I mean.

"Detective Clayton will be with you in a few minutes."

I imagined that my father waited for half an hour. I know that I sat in the car for half an hour before I finally got out and walked up to the police station. I wandered around the building until I finally stumbled upon my father, sitting alone and quiet.

"I told you to wait in the car," he said.

"It's too cold."

He nodded his head. He understood. He almost always did.

"Why's it taking so long?" I asked.

"Don't know."

Just then a white man in a suit walked up to us.

"Hello," he said. "I'm Detective Clayton."

The detective offered his hand to my father and my father took it. They shook hands quickly, formally. The detective sat down behind the desk, ruffled through a few sheets of paper, and looked hard at both of us. Looked at me as if I might have answers. Of course, I didn't. But he gave me a look up and down, just in case. Or maybe he always looked at people that way, with those detective eyes. I wouldn't want to be his son. Just as much as I wouldn't want my father to be an undertaker or astronaut. The undertaker's eyes always look like they're measuring you for a coffin and the astronaut's eyes are always looking up into the sky. My father was mostly unemployed. His eyes had stories written across them.

Anyway, the detective looked at his papers some more. Then he cleared his throat.

"I'm sure you know why you're here," he said to my father.

"It's about Jerry Vincent."

"Yes, it is. And I see here that you've been questioned about this before."

"Annually," my father said.

"Do you have anything new to add?"

"I've told you guys everything I know about what happened."

"And nothing has changed? You haven't remembered something different, some detail you may have forgotten?"

"Nothing."

The detective wrote for a while, his tongue poking out of his mouth a little. Like a little kid. Like I did when I was six, seven, and eight years old. I laughed.

"What's so funny?" the detective and my father asked me. They were both smiling.

I shook my head and laughed harder. Soon all three of us were laughing, at mostly nothing. Maybe we were all nervous or bored. Or both. The detective opened his desk drawer, pulled out a piece of hard candy, and handed it to me.

"There you go," he said.

I looked at the candy for a while and gave it to my father. He looked at it for a while, too, and handed it back to the detective.

"I'm sorry, Detective Clayton," my father said. "But my son and I are diabetics."

"Oh, sorry," the detective said and looked at us with sad eyes. Especially at me. Juvenile diabetes. A tough life. I learned how to use a hypodermic needle before I could ride a bike. I lost more of my own blood to glucose tests than I ever did to childhood accidents.

"Nothing to be sorry for," my father said. "It's under control."

The detective looked at us both like he didn't believe it. All he knew was criminals and how they worked. He must have figured diabetes worked like a criminal, breaking and entering. But he had it wrong. Diabetes is just like a lover, hurting you from the inside. I was closer to my diabetes than to any of my

221

family or friends. Even when I was all alone, quiet, thinking, wanting no company at all, my diabetes was there. That's the truth.

"Well," the detective said. "I don't think I have anything else to ask you. But if you remember anything else, make sure you contact me."

"Okay," my father said and we stood up. The detective and my father shook hands again.

"Was Jerry Vincent your friend?" the detective asked.

"He still is," my father said.

My father and I walked out of the police station, feeling guilty. I kept wondering if they knew I shoplifted a deck of cards from Sears when I was ten years old. Or if they knew that I once beat up a little kid for the fun of it. Or if they knew I stole my cousin's bike and wrecked it on purpose. Kept wrecking it until it was useless.

Anyway, my father and I walked to the car, climbed in, and pulled out of the parking lot.

"Ready to head home?" he asked.

"Been ready."

There wasn't much to say during the drive back to the reservation. I mean, Jerry Vincent was gone. What more could I ask my father about him? At what point do we just re-create the people who have disappeared from our lives? Jerry Vincent might have been a mean drunk. He might have had stinky feet and a bad haircut. Nobody talks about that kind of stuff. He was almost a hero now, Jerry Vincent, who probably got shot in the head and might be buried somewhere in Manito Park. Sometimes it seems like all Indians can do is talk about the disappeared.

My father got completely out of control once because he lost the car keys. Explain that to a sociologist.

It was dark by the time we got home. Mom had fry bread and chili waiting for us. My sisters and brothers were all home, watching television, playing cards. Believe me. When we got home everybody was there, everybody. My father sat at the table and nearly cried into his food. Then, of course, he did cry into his food and we all watched him. All of us.

FLIGHT

John-John had been saving dollar bills toward a dream and when he had a shoebox full of bills he sat down to count out his future. "One, two, three," he counted, all the way up to ten to make a neat stack on the floor, and soon he had two hundred neat stacks in exact rows and columns.

How much is enough?

John-John packed a suitcase with his dollar bills, a change of underwear, a toothbrush, and a photograph of his older brother, Joseph. The photograph was folded, spindled, mutilated. Joseph, the jet pilot, sat in full military dress in front of an American flag.

Dear Mr. and Mrs. _____, we regret to inform you that your son, _____, was shot down and taken prisoner by the enemy during a routine military operation. At this time, we are doing everything within our power to assure the immediate and safe release of your son.

Sincerely, they said.

John-John remembered the world before, remembered the four walls and one window of the HUD house on the reservation. So most Indians had no job and they counted change to buy the next bottle of wine. Maybe the wells went dry every summer and maybe any water still left was too radioactive to drink.

"Uranium has a half-life of one hundred thirty-five million years," somebody told Joseph, and he said, "Shit, I can tell you stories that will last longer than that."

Then there was music.

Joseph sang in a voice so pure even the drunkest Indians threw their bottles down. He sang in a voice so sharp even the oldest Indians could hear him clearly. He sang in a voice so deep even the whitest Indians remembered the words.

Sometimes, he danced.

Joseph had big feet and he stumbled, often lost the rhythm of drums. But he smiled and picked himself up from the ground after he fell. He whistled. He slapped his thighs. He crow-hopped and sprained his ankle. He danced.

Joseph paid the rent.

*   *   *

After Joseph was taken as a prisoner of war, John-John waited at the window for years. He ate and drank at that window; he slept with his eyes open. John-John's friends grew up, graduated or dropped out of school, married, had children, got drunk too much, but he stood there at the window and waited.

John-John remembered: the sky and ground disappeared into the horizon, that imaginary line forever rolling away. Snow. Ice. Cold wind. Joseph in blue parka and military-surplus boots. After Christmas but before New Year's Eve. Everyone was sober. Standing in some anonymous field while his Chevy sat a few feet away on the other side of a fence, Joseph raised his arms and said, *Someday, the world will be mine.* Maybe he just said, *Goddamn, I need a drink.* Joseph had already dug through the ashtray, in the glove compartment, under seats. There was no money left in the world. Not even loose coins. *We ain't got gas and I'm out of miracles,* Joseph said and walked fifteen miles for help.

Now John-John stood on the front porch with his suitcase, a key hanging on a string around his neck. No lock, no door. The key was just a small mystery. It didn't fit any lock on the reservation. Maybe it opened a garage door in Seattle; maybe it started a car in Spokane.

John-John watched the sky for signs, read the sun for the correct time, and checked his watch to be sure. *It's time to go,* he thought just as the jet ripped through the sound barrier and shook the air. John-John tumbled down the stairs, landed on his tailbone. He stood up, rubbed his ass, and searched the sky for evidence. He could see vapor trails stretched across the sky.

John-John ran for the football field, down the reservation highway, three miles of smooth, smooth pavement. It happens that way: the tribe had a government grant to fix the roads, but half the Indians on the reservation still lived on commodities. John-John ran until his chest hurt and legs trembled. He ran to the end of the highway and stared back toward his house, at the jet approaching, then landing with a concussion of noise.

The jet taxied down the highway, turbines slowing, and came to a stop a few feet from John-John. Power. Heat. Noise. It all felt and sounded like possibilities; it was the machinery of dreams. John-John stared at the jet until it grew beyond his vision. His eyes watered, ached. He rubbed at them with fists until they grew out of proportion. Minutes went by until the jet was silent in the silence its arrival created.

Has Christopher Columbus come back?

John-John walked toward the jet, slowly, carefully. His steps were measured and precise. Step on a crack, break your mother's back. A balance beam is only four inches wide; the reservation is only half that width. John-John reached out and touched the jet with a fingertip. Hot and cold. He jumped back as the cockpit opened and a voice called out.

"Sir, ace jet pilot Joseph Victor, code name Geronimo, reporting for duty, sir!"

A tall man climbed down from the cockpit and stood at attention. His unbraided hair fell out from under his flight helmet, reached down to the small of his back. The tall man saluted John-John, then wheeled and saluted the crowd of Indians quickly gathering. He turned back to John-John.

"Sir, may I have permission to remove my helmet, sir?"

John-John was stunned. He raised his arm in a half-salute, the heels of his tennis shoes clicked together.

"Joseph, is that you?"

"Sir, yes, sir. May I please remove my helmet, sir?"

"Yeah, go ahead."

Joseph removed his helmet, leaned it against a hip, still at attention. His face was scarred, battered. The purple scar between his eyes was shaped like a cigar butt; the symmetrical scars up and down his cheeks looked like gills.

"Joseph, your face. What happened?"

John-John moved closer to his brother, reached out and touched the scars, the skin. Hot and cold. Both close to tears.

"Sir, it's been a long and glorious war but I am happy to be home, sir."

"But your face. What did they do to you?"

"Sir, I am proud to say I withstood their tortures with courage and strength. I only gave them my name, rank, and serial number, sir."

John-John cried then, took his brother's hand. Swollen and scratched, Joseph's hand felt like fear and failure. He had lost his left ring finger, his nails were torn, some missing altogether. Crude initials were carved into his palms.

"Joseph, don't you recognize me? It's your brother John-John."

Joseph stared at his brother intently, searched his memory. He saw those eyes curved like a bow, colored like the center of the earth; that hair short and still untamed, black; that mouth, too small for the face; those teeth yellowed and healthy; those hands, that hand now holding his, so long and forgiving, skin like a woman's.

Who are you? Who are you?

"Sir, I don't remember. I'm sorry. I just don't remember, sir."

228

Memory, like a coin trick, like the French drop with one hand passing over the other, quarter dropping out of sight, then out of existence. *It was there! It was there!* The little Indian boys screaming at the sudden recognition of their first metaphor. Memory like an abandoned car, rusting and forgotten though it sits in plain view for decades. Dogs have litters there; generations of spiders live a terrible history. All of it goes unnoticed and no one bothers to tell the story.

This is not the story John-John tells himself just before he falls asleep. In his story, Joseph comes back on a bus, on a train, hitchhiking. In his story, Joseph's feet never leave the ground again. But that kind of vision is costly; it rips sweat from John-John's sleep and skin. He wakes up with a thirst that is so large that nothing can be forgiven. He wakes up with the sound of Joseph's voice in his nose. Reverberation.

"Hey, John-John, why do you got two first names?"

"'Cuz you have to say anything twice to make it true?"

"No, that ain't it."

"'Cuz our parents really meant it when they named me?"

"I don't think so."

"Maybe it's just a memory device?"

"Who knows?"

Joseph sitting at the kitchen table as they replay this conversation, this way of greeting, each day. Ever since John-John could form a sentence, Joseph began the morning with the same question.

"Hey, John-John, why do you got two first names?"

"'Cuz I'm supposed to be twins?"

"No, man, that's too easy."

"'Cuz Mother always had a stutter?"

Laugher. Then more laughter. Then coffee and buttered toast. Sometimes, a day-old doughnut. The sun came in through the windows. It was there, just as much as the tablecloth or the salt and pepper shakers.

Hey, John-John, why do you got two first names?

Now John-John waiting at the window. Watching. Telling the glass his stories, whispering to the pane, his breath fogging the world. His house, his family's house, closed in all around him. Too many photographs. Too many stray papers and tattered magazines. The carpet has fleas.

There have been smaller disasters.

Mother and father, sister and sister, rush, rush. Fumigate, bleach and vinegar in the laundry, old blankets driven to the dump. The dog, lonely and confused, chained to a spare tire in the yard.

"John-John," his mother says. "You have to leave. I mean, we all have to leave the house for a few hours. It'll be toxic for a while, you know?"

He is dragged from the window, sat down beside the dog on the lawn. They both howl.

Once, John-John dreamed of flight. He imagined a crazed run into the forest, into the pine. Maybe then they would search for him, search for Joseph out there in the dark. John-John wanted to build fires with no flame or smoke. He wanted to hide in the brush while searchers walked by, inches away, calling out his name. He wanted helicopters with spotlights, all-terrain vehicles, the local news.

230

Together, they would lift stones and find Joseph; they would shake trees and Joseph would fall to the ground; they would drink Joseph from their canteens; they would take photographs of Joseph crawling like a bear across snow, stunned by winter. The rescue team would find John-John and Joseph huddled together like old men, like children, like small birds tensing their bodies for flight.

John-John sits at his window. Waits. Watches. His face touches the glass. Hot and cold. His eyes follow the vapor trails that appear in the reservation sky. They are ordinary and magical.

Next time, John-John thinks. *Next time, it will be Joseph.*

Maybe it is winter again. Maybe it is just summer disguised. There is no one left to notice. Dust. Cold wind. Noise. John-John hears it all in his head. He counts his dollar bills, *one, two, three,* all the way up to ten before he starts again. He waits; he watches.

He wants to escape.

JUNIOR POLATKIN'S WILD WEST SHOW

In the dream he sometimes had, Junior Polatkin would be a gunfighter. A gunfighter with braids and a ribbon shirt. He wouldn't speak English, just whisper Spokane as he gunned down Wild Bill Hickok, Bat Masterson, even Billy the Kid. Junior dreamed his name would be Sonny Six-Gun and he dreamed that white and Indian people would sing ballads about him.

But Junior always had to wake up, stagger from bed, and make his way to his first class at Gonzaga University in Spokane, Washington. Junior was the only Indian at Gonzaga, a small Jesuit school originally founded to educate the local tribes. Now, it catered to upper-middle-class white kids running away from their parents. Hardly anybody was actually from around Spokane. The students were from California, Montana, Hawaii.

"Everywhere but here," Junior said to himself often. "Anywhere but here."

As he sat in his history class on the first day of December, Junior watched the beautiful blond woman who sat in the front row. Now, Junior would never have called her beautiful. That was a word he couldn't really relate to. No, he would've called her pretty, nice-looking, maybe even attractive. But more than her looks, Junior liked the way she talked, how she continually challenged the professor's lecture points. Everyone else in the class grumbled when the blonde raised her hand to speak, but Junior leaned forward to be sure to hear every word she said.

"Yes, Lynn." The professor recognized the blonde and took a deep breath.

"Don't you think we spend too much time mythologizing the West? I mean, look at how it really was. Dirty, violent, illiterate. It wasn't an age for heroes, that's for sure."

The professor ignored Lynn's comments and proceeded with his lecture. Junior nearly fell in love at that moment. At least, he fell in love with the idea of falling in love with Lynn, and that's powerful medicine in itself. Junior spent the rest of the class watching Lynn and dreaming.

After class, he followed Lynn to the cafeteria, stayed just a few steps behind her. He thought he was being a good Indian, sneaky and all, but she suddenly turned around and confronted him.

"What the fuck do you want?" Lynn asked.

Junior couldn't think of a thing to say, had no quick and clever response, no words that would convey what he felt. He'd waited for this moment for most of the semester, had dreamed of it, had nearly lived it in his imagination, and now he was silent.

"Well," Lynn asked again. "What the fuck do you want?"

Junior searched his mind and pockets, tried to remember some stunning piece of poetry from his English class or a line of dialogue from a romantic movie. He licked his lips, cleared his throat.

"Coffee," he said and exhaled heavily, as if he had just changed the world.

"What?" Lynn asked, surprised.

"Just coffee," Junior said, then amended himself. "Just going, cafeteria, coffee."

Lynn looked hard at Junior, dismissed him as a threat, and continued her walk to the cafeteria. Junior waited until she was a good distance ahead and followed her, wondered if there was a bigger asshole in the world than he was.

"Nope, I'm the biggest," he said to himself as he walked into the cafeteria and took a seat as far as possible from where Lynn sat.

"Can I help you?" the waiter asked, suddenly appearing, as good waiters will do.

"Coffee," Junior said. "Just coffee."

Over Christmas break, Junior lived in the dorms because he didn't want to go back to his reservation and endure the insults that would be continually hurled at him. Instead, he stayed in the dorms by himself and read books. Nearly a book a day. On Christmas, Junior read two books, switched back and forth by chapters. One book was a cheap western and the other was a children's book. He pretended it was one big book, a strange book, a multiple-personality book. After a while, he switched back and forth by paragraph:

234

Johnny Star stared out over the edge of the cliff and watched Bull Steedham ride his beautiful horse. *That man is too ugly to have a horse that pretty,* Johnny thought as he balanced his six-gun on his left forearm, took aim at Bull's hat, and pulled the trigger.

It was a rainy day on Bobby's street. It was a rainy day. Bobby put on his yellow rain slicker and his yellow rain boots and went out into the rain to play. It rained all day. Bobby splashed through puddles and pretended to be a sailor. It was rainy, rainy day and Bobby pretended to sail away.

Junior read his books and stared out his window into the snow. He watched cars pass by and wondered if white people were happier than Indians. He figured that even white people can't be happy at all the time but they must be happier most of the time. At least, they must spend more time being happy than Indians do.

Junior checked his mail three times a day although the mail was only delivered at ten in the morning. There would be letters from his family out on the reservation. Merry Christmas and a Happy New Year. That kind of thing. Junior always half-expected a little miracle in the mail. After all, it was the season for miracles. But nothing ever happened until December 29, a day that is marked by nothing.

On that day, Junior went to check his mail for the second time and discovered Lynn, the woman from his history class, checking her mail.

"Hey," she asked. "Weren't you in my history class?"

"Yeah," Junior said and wondered if she remembered their brief conversation outside the cafeteria.

"What did you think?" she asked.

"It was all right."

"Did you get a good grade?"

"It was all right."

She smiled and looked at Junior, hoped he would continue the conversation, introduce a new topic, tell a joke, something. She had been a little lonely, living in the dorm over the holidays.

"Indian," Junior suddenly said with great passion, as if he were running for office.

"What?" Lynn asked and laughed.

"Indian," Junior repeated. "I'm Indian."

"Yeah, I know," she said.

Junior looked down at his shoes, tugged at his shirt, ran his fingers through his hair. Lynn stared at him, smiled, but Junior couldn't maintain eye contact.

"You're pretty quiet," she said.

"Yeah, sometimes, but not always."

"What's your name?"

"Polatkin. Junior Polatkin."

"I'm Casey. Lynn Casey. Pleased to meet you."

They shook hands, then, standing by the mailboxes. Junior started to feel more comfortable and Lynn did most of the talking anyway, so they moved the conversation from the dorm to the student lounge, and then ended up at a restaurant just off campus.

"So, what's it like being the only Indian here?" Lynn asked.

"It gets pretty lonely, you know? I've got friends but I don't ever feel like I fit in."

"Do you drink much?"

"What do you mean?"

"Well," Lynn said. "I've seen you before. At parties and stuff. You seem to drink a lot."

"Yeah, I guess. Maybe I drink a lot."

Junior couldn't believe she was asking him these personal questions. She hardly knew him but it didn't seem wrong. Somehow or other, Junior trusted Lynn immediately.

"Well, I'm not passing judgment or anything," Lynn said. "I'm just curious. I remember you from class, too. You were always late."

"I don't like waking up much."

"Yeah, me neither."

Junior and Lynn shared an order of french fries and talked for hours. Junior had probably seen too many movies in his life, so he imagined their conversation was a movie. He imagined that Mel Gibson would play him and Kim Basinger would play Lynn. But he changed his mind. He wanted this movie to be classic, to be the best movie put to film. It would star Robert De Niro and Meryl Streep. And in a real character stretch, De Niro would play Lynn and Meryl would play him, complete with reservation accent.

"What are you laughing about?" Lynn asked Junior and he told her his plans for casting the movie.

"De Niro?" Lynn asked. "You think De Niro could play me?"

"De Niro can play anybody." Junior said.

"You know what? I think it should be made into a western, staring Clint Eastwood and Sigourney Weaver."

"Hey," Junior said. "I thought you didn't like westerns."

Lynn laughed and looked at Junior, studied his features. He had long hair, not as long as some Indians, but definitely longer than the hair of all the nice Catholic boys at Gonzaga. He had a

237

nice, open face. Not handsome, really, but definitely not plain. It was his hands that were beautiful. He made strange, unexpected gestures when he talked, used his hands like a magician would.

"Your hands are beautiful," Lynn said.

"Really?" Junior asked, surprised. He looked at his own hands as if they belonged to someone else. They had never been more than tools to him. Now maybe they were beautiful tools.

"Hi," Junior said instead of thanking Lynn for her compliment. He became very nervous.

"Hi," Lynn said.

They sat there for a little while longer in silence. Then Lynn paid for the food and led Junior out the door.

"Listen," she said and kissed Junior. Just like that, they kissed. Junior had never kissed a white woman before and he used his tongue a lot, reached for every part of her mouth, and tried to find out if she tasted different.

"Irish," Lynn broke the kiss and said, as if she read Junior's mind. "I'm Irish."

Junior dreamed of the western that starred Lynn as Lynn and Junior as himself. During the love scenes, the camera would fade out just as they fell into each other's arms. But in real life, Junior and Lynn fell onto the bed, drew circles on each other's naked bodies, and counted moles.

Junior ran through his vocabulary in his mind: make love, sex, do it, fuck. He wanted to climb out of bed and find a thesaurus. He wanted Lynn to whisper synonyms in his ear.

Lynn touched Junior's brown skin and smiled. She realized that all those sexual stereotypes about Indians were both true and

238

false, but then she also realized that there were no sexual stereotypes about Indians. She touched her belly and wondered if she had gotten pregnant. They had used a rubber but who knows about those things, right? She rubbed her belly a little and wondered what their imaginary baby would look like. She was almost scared. She hadn't meant this to happen, she'd just wanted some company. She'd never been alone at Christmas. Junior was Santa Claus with braids, maybe.

"What if I'm pregnant?"

"You're not."

"Maybe I am."

"Maybe not."

But Lynn missed her next period and then her next before she went to student health to confirm the news. Junior waited for her outside, in the snow and cold.

"I'm pregnant," she said.

"What do you want to do?"

She shrugged her shoulders.

"Get married?" Junior asked.

"No," she said. "I don't love you. It was just one night."

"Abortion?"

"No way, I'd go to hell for sure. I'm Catholic, remember?"

"Adoption?"

"I couldn't give my baby away after carrying it all that time."

"Our baby," Junior said. "*Our* baby."

Lynn started to cry and Junior soon joined her. They walked for hours, talked very little.

"Oh, God, what's he going to be?" Lynn said. "What should we name him?"

"She," Junior said. "Maybe it'll be a she."

*   *   *

Sean Casey was a healthy baby, with dark skin and blue eyes, webbed toes. He could talk by the time he was one and read by the time he was three. But Junior only learned those details through the mail, by random phone calls and timed visits. He had never pressed Lynn for anything other than minimal visitation rights and Lynn loved him for that small act, if nothing else.

Lynn's parents refused to accept Sean Casey's Indian blood and, in fact, exhibited a kind of denial that was nearly pathological in its intensity. But Lynn continually reminded Sean of his heritage, read him books about Indians in the womb and crib, gave him Indian books to read when he finally could do it himself.

Lynn taught Sean the Spokane word for love, *quen comanche*, but Sean could never get his tongue around the syllables. But he always tried.

Lynn eventually returned to Gonzaga after dropping out to have the baby. Junior always imagined that in their movie, she would have a one-paragraph description of the rest of her life just before the closing credits rolled:

> LYNN CASEY returned to college and earned her degree in American History. She graduated with honors and is currently pursuing her master's in history, focusing on the American West. Her thesis paper, "Of Bullets and Band-Aids: Repairing the Mythology of Dodge City," is being published in the *Journal of Applied History and Literature*, Summer 1986. Lynn and her son, Sean, live in Spokane, Washington.

Junior stayed in school another year, even took another history class from the professor who'd taught that course where Lynn and Junior had met. Although Junior had done fairly well in the first class, he wanted to do even better the next time around. He studied hard, sacrificed his grades in other courses, even skipped other classes to study history. And just like Lynn had done, he challenged the professor on every point. Every detail.

"But don't you think the gunfighter was just a symbol that justified the violent nature of white men?" Junior asked.

The professor ignored Junior and continued with his lecture. Junior leaned back in his chair and dreamed of being a gunfighter. He drew his pistol and fired, once, twice, three times. He never missed.

"But don't you think the western movie is just a contemporary measure of America's fondness for war?" Junior asked.

"Okay, okay," the professor said. "Enough lecture. Time for a pop quiz. And you can all thank Mr. Polatkin for it."

The class groaned and struggled with the test. Junior ran through the test, answered most questions correctly, missed a couple. He carried the test up to the professor.

"Correct this," Junior said.

"I'll give it back to you next class," the professor said.

"No, correct it now."

The professor grabbed the test from Junior, hoped it was a failure. But Junior did well enough to get an A.

"Happy now?" the professor asked.

"No," Junior said. He took the test paper back and threw it in the garbage as he walked out the classroom door and out of college. He hitchhiked back to the reservation, stopped at a pay phone, and made a collect call to Lynn.

"Hello, Lynn, this is Junior. I left school."

"Junior, you can't do that. You can't go back to the reservation. You'll die out there."

"Well, I'm dying at school, too. So I guess it's a matter of choosing my own grave."

"Listen, Junior, do you need anything?"

"Can I talk to my son?"

"Sure, hold on."

Junior waited for Sean Casey's voice.

"Hello?"

"Hi, Sean, it's Daddy."

"Daddy."

"I love you, Sean."

"*Quen comanche*, Daddy."

"Yeah, Sean, *quen comanche*."

Junior hung up the phone and walked down the highway toward the reservation. He wanted to imagine that he was walking off into the sunset, into a happy ending. But he knew that all along the road he traveled, there were reservation drive-ins, each showing a new and painful sequel to the first act of his life.

The Lone Ranger and Tonto Fistfight in Heaven

Sherman Alexie

ABOUT THIS GUIDE

We hope that these discussion questions
will enhance your reading group's exploration of
The Lone Ranger and Tonto Fistfight in Heaven. They are
meant to stimulate discussion,
offer new viewpoints, and enrich your enjoyment
of the book.

More reading group guides and additional information,
including summaries, author tours, and author sites, for
other fine Grove/Atlantic titles, may be found on
our Web site, www.groveatlantic.com.

QUESTIONS FOR DISCUSSION

by Carol Rawlings-Miller

1. Epigrams from Lou Reed and Joy Harjo prepare the reader's way into the collection. What ideas do they set in motion that the stories build? What do they reflect about Sherman Alexie's sensibility?

2. Throughout the opening story, "Every Little Hurricane," literal and figurative references to weather weave together: there is, in fact, a storm and in the lives of the characters there is volatility, too. Tension builds between the characters and erupts violently as the storm moves through. What is created through this interworking of the literal and figurative? Through the close connecting of the natural and the human worlds?

3. In "Every Little Hurricane," as two brothers fight and nearly murder each other, characters watch rather than act to avert a tragedy. Why don't they intervene? Is it merely a matter of passivity? What is meant by the line "This little kind of hurricane was generic"?

4. Thomas Builds-the-Fire, the seer, becomes increasingly isolated as the stories progress. Victor says, "Hell, he looked around our world and then poked his head through some hole in the wall into another world. A better world." Even so, Victor asks him if he really believes that shit, and others, too, resist and mock his visions. Why? How would you characterize his visions, his place on the reservation, and the nature of the threat that he poses?

5. Victor's relationship with tradition (and Thomas) is complex. After he calls Thomas's visions "that shit," Thomas walks away from him—for several years, as it turns out. Big Ma, the spiritual leader of the Spokanes, gives Victor a drum—a pager, she jokes. Victor calls it the "only religion I have." What is Victor's relationship with religion and tradition? Why does he have a sudden need for tradition when his father dies? When they discuss tossing the ashes of Victor's father into the Spokane Falls, Thomas imagines him rising like a salmon and Victor imagines him cleaning the attic. What do these different visions reflect about them?

6. The deep longing of young men to be warriors emerges in several stories. Why? What is the particular freight of this desire for young Indian men? What fuels their desire? What frustrates its fulfillment?

7. In "The Only Traffic Signal on the Reservation" Alexie depicts baseball as having extraordinary significance on the reservation. With what meaning(s) is baseball invested? Why?

8. An epigram from Kafka's *The Trial* introduces "The Trials of Thomas Builds-the-Fire." What tone does the quotation set? Kafka's sensibility, his nightmarish evocation of modern life, has inspired writers from diverse traditions. Why might Kafka be a potent reference point for Alexie? Why *The Trial* in particular?

9. "Distances" is a vision of Thomas's that is framed at the culmination of "The Trials of Thomas Builds-the-Fire," which is in itself a blend of the fantastic and the real. As we move ever more deeply into the place of vision, do we feel that we are moving away from the truth? Or closer to it? How does Alexie depict the Tribal Council? What is being explored?

10. In "Distances" the line "I dreamed of television and woke up crying" is set off and repeated. What is the importance of this line? How does it compare to the line repeated in "The Love Song of J. Alfred Prufrock": "In the room the women come and go / Talking of Michelangelo"? How does Alexie's line connect to the rest of the story, to its tone? How does it relate to Thomas's vision of the Tribal Council? What would the story be like without it?

11. Profound complexities attend the characters' lives, saddled as they are with the weight of a tragic history and the difficulties of modern Indian life. "Imagining the Reservation" ends with a series of sentences that begin imperatively—"Imagine." What does Alexie suggest about the force and potential of the imagination for Indians?

12. In "The Approximate Size of My Favorite Tumor" Alexie calls humor "an antiseptic that cleaned out the deepest personal wounds." How important is humor in *The Lone Ranger and Tonto Fistfight in Heaven*? What sort of humor prevails?

13. Throughout the stories Alexie vividly evokes the fragility of the tribal world. There is a sense that the tribe threatens to die out: "Sometimes it feels like our tribe is dying a piece of fry bread at a time." How does this sense of threat to the culture affect the lives of the characters? How does it inform the tone of *The Lone Ranger and Tonto Fistfight in Heaven*?

14. Early in "Witnesses, Secret and Not" the narrator tells a story from the time when he was thirteen. He refers to the challenge of figuring out what it means to be Indian. In "Witness" he goes with his father when he is called in for questioning about an old case that involves a missing Indian. We hear that "sometimes it seems that all Indians can do is talk about the disappeared." Why are the disappeared discussed? How does this connect to the question of Indian identity articulated early in the story?

15. In his stories Alexie frequently includes details of everyday contemporary life, with its Diet Pepsis and 7-Elevens. Why? What do these details contribute to the tone and texture of the stories?

16. On the other hand, Sherman Alexie's use of language can trope toward the poetic, becoming lush, or sparklingly vivid, or hauntingly rhythmic. Why do his stories accommodate such play with language? When does his writing tend to become more poetic?

17. For viewers of *Smoke Signals*, how well do you think the movie captures the quality of the narratives in *The Lone Ranger and Tonto Fistfight in Heaven*?

18. Throughout these stories characters drink and are drunk. As Alexie acknowledges in his Introduction, he has been criticized for promoting the stereotype of the drunk Indian. How just is this critique? What does his underscoring of the force of drink in Indian life say about his sensibility as a writer?

19. In his Introduction Sherman Alexie confesses the largely autobiographical nature of these stories, but he also asserts that they really are not true. They are the vision of "one individual looking at the lives of his family and his entire tribe, so these stories are necessarily biased, incomplete, exaggerated, deluded, and often just plain wrong. But in trying to make them true and real, I am writing what might be called reservation realism." He doesn't explain "reservation realism," but rather points to the stories and instructs the reader "to figure that out for yourself." What, in fact, do you think he means by "reservation realism"?

20. Why do you think *The Lone Ranger and Tonto Fistfight in Heaven* has become a significant book? Are these stories important as an evocation not only of Indian life, but of American life as well?

Sherman Alexie is the author of *Reservation Blues, Indian Killer, The Toughest Indian in the World,* and *Ten Little Indians.* He wrote and directed *The Business of Fancydancing* and also wrote the award-winning screenplay for *Smoke Signals,* a film based on his short-story collection *The Lone Ranger and Tonto Fistfight in Heaven.* His books have won numerous awards and have been selected from *People*'s "Best of" pages and *The New York Times* Notable Books of the Year.